EUROPA28

First published in Great Britain in 2020 by Comma Press.
commapress.co.uk

A CIP catalogue record of this book is available from the British Library.

ISBN: 1-912697-29-7
ISBN-13: 978-1-91269-729-8

The European Commission's support for the production of this publication does
not constitute an endorsement of the contents, which reflect the views only of the
authors, and the Commission cannot be held responsible for any use which may be
made of the information contained therein.

The publisher gratefully acknowledges assistance from Arts Council England.

Printed and bound in England by Clays Ltd, Elcograf S.p.A

EUROPA28

Writing by Women on the Future of Europe

Edited by Sophie Hughes
& Sarah Cleave

Contents

CONTENTS

CONTENTS

Introduction

WOMEN SEE THINGS DIFFERENTLY. Of course we do. Like anybody, we bring our own unique experiences to our perception of any problem. The rich and detailed tapestry of who we are is made up of every moment we have lived, felt, seen, experienced, suffered. It affects the way we see things. And we cannot look through anybody else's eyes but our own.

Usually, we don't think much about how differently people see things. We accept 'home truths', or conventional wisdom. We come to believe that the certainties presented by the loudest voices are irreproachable: that the narrative presented to us as 'the state of Europe' today is fact.

So it might come as a shock, between the covers of this book, to look at our world only through women's eyes. To see a Europe so far removed from the over-simplistic, binary, staid portrayal of recent times. To come to it afresh in all its fractured, fragile, compromised, contoured parts. To recognise its flaws and its richness, its gifts and its costs, its challenges and its beauty. Like this, in the words of Asja Bakić, 'It looks... fragile'.

It also looks like hope.

We cannot rebuild what we cannot clearly see. We cannot challenge invisible injustices, nor hope to heal wounds we are not brave enough to inspect. We cannot solve a problem without a name, nor address the needs of a shapeless group of people we vaguely label 'left behind' because we are too lazy ever to find out who they are.

To take stock of where we are, and to move forward, we need new ways of seeing the world around us. New ways to look at Europe and the world beyond, and a willingness to forge new ways of being in that world. As Hilary Cottam writes: 'The answers perhaps lie in a different kind of thinking – or magic if you will.'

Through women's eyes, we can begin to see things differently. It comes as a shock, because our default setting is to see things through men's eyes without even realising we are doing so. The front pages that deliver us our daily bulletins, the think tanks that advise us, the politicians pontificating and talking heads tattling: they seem to provide us such wide-ranging perspectives. But we are hearing from the same people over and over again. Not just because their views are so frequently informed by the same socio-economic, geographical, ethnic and educational background. But because, in UK Parliamentary debates about Brexit, for example, 90 per cent of the talking is done by men.[1]

As any Instagram aficionado will attest, when you have looked at something through a single filter for long enough, it can be a shock to switch to a fresh lens. What is presented to us as real might be hopelessly distorted by airbrushing, but when it is all we see, it quickly becomes accepted as the truth. Like the 'carefully created but unreal image' from Nora Ikstena's story, in which the eyes of a young Europa are brutally opened to a new reality. For a continent named after the myth of a rape, to be forced to look anew at itself through women's eyes is a refreshing and necessary concept.

'What European society so desperately needs nowadays,' writes Apolena Rychlíková, 'is a chance to take a deep breath and start thinking beyond the present day, a chance to see itself in a different way, in a different constellation and social order.'

Looking at the world through different eyes is a challenge and it can feel like an affront. The pieces of writing contained in this book are not always easy to read. They are exacting, challenging and complex. As any good solution should be. They encourage us to look at Europe with a fresh perspective, to question our own assumptions and the limitations of what we have thought possible.

They dare us to move away from a hard and dry consideration of economic factors, of numbers and currency and market movements, and to think instead as people. To think afresh, in the language of Janne Teller's 'livability' – of community – of the simple yearning for what Apolena Rychlíková describes as 'a dignified and well-rounded life'.

We cannot achieve a future of peace and prosperity without confronting the sins of the past. These women encourage us to acknowledge our own failings and wrongdoing: to examine, for example, what Gloria Wekker describes as 'the utter lack of shame manifesting in European political attitudes towards the non-European Other during the colonial era and now.' Renata Salecl gives us the uncomfortable task of recognising ourselves as a version of the anti-vaxxer, reliant on the tendency of others to make less selfish choices in order that we might pursue our own ruthless individualism. These writers hold up a mirror that is not easy to look into.

Again and again in these pieces, the question of gaze emerges. Where do we choose to look? And when do we allow ourselves to avert our eyes? Will we choose to confront the urgency of climate disaster, or bury our heads in the sand until it is too late? Are we brave enough to look directly at the devastating chasm between our richest and poorest citizens and to admit the hard realities that have widened it? Can we continue to witness the deaths of innocent people at our borders with little more than curious detachment as they beg us to let them in? 'How humiliating and how tragic,' as Leila Slimani says.

None of this is easy. As Tereza Nvotová writes, it will require *persistence*. Or, as Edurne Portela explains, it might only be achieved if we are forced, literally, to stumble over painful reminders of past resistance in order to write a different kind of future for ourselves.

It will also require us to join forces. Nowhere before reading the pieces contained in *Europa28* have I experienced quite this exhilarating mixture of politics with science, philosophy with economics, ethics with architecture. We have a modern tendency to approach a problem from a single angle. To drill down ever deeper into narrow solutions based in a single discipline. But just as the peoples and countries of Europe are not a homogenous bloc, and yet have come together to create something with its own identity, its own magic, so it might take a little of the power of each of these different ways of seeing the world to find our path. We will need both fact and fiction, if we are to admit to the reality of our situation, and yet still have the audacity to dream a new way of being.

If we are to realise the promise offered by female thinkers, we must also ask difficult questions. It is one thing to celebrate women's ideas and advances, and another to do the necessary work to enable them to come to fruition. Are we prepared to make the required cultural and structural shifts to clear a path for the women like those whose words appear in this volume? Will we enable them to fulfil their potential contribution to our shared future?

For too long, we have demanded that women themselves do the work of dismantling their own oppression, a clever trap which pays lip service to awareness of the problem whilst re-burdening its victims still further. What glorious contributions to our society, culture, politics and technology have been suppressed or lost because of the sheer amount of time, energy and headspace taken up with recovering from harassment, avoiding predators, and nursing trauma? What treasures have we robbed ourselves of while we loaded women with abuse upon abuse, piling the indignities up higher and higher until their hands were so full that other things began to fall out?

Will we be brave? Will we be honest? Will we find a way to listen? Will we look at ourselves? They are not easy actions to take but women like these are ready to lead the way, if we will let them. We are not led by women, however. Our parliaments lack them: their voices and their wisdom, their perspectives and their passion, their ability to step across divides and find familiar, shared ground. We punish them, we shut them out and we sorely feel their missing presence. Women of colour, trans women, disabled women, poor women, most of all. The voices we most need to hear are the ones we ostracise and abuse. Yet we have painted ourselves into a corner, with our standard-issue paintbrushes. The solution must be creative. We will need different minds and new stories in order to move forward.

Will we find them?

Gloria Wekker writes: 'The issue, finally, is whether we allow our basest fears and anxieties to define who we are as Europeans.' With the benefit of new and diverse perspectives, the courage to confront our own culpability, and the determination to challenge the barriers of inequality, a future Europe might be defined by our greatest hopes instead.

Laura Bates
London, October 2019

Note

1. https://www.theneweuropean.co.uk/top-stories/womens-voices-not-being-heard-in-brexit-debate-say-peoples-vote-campaigners-1-5734570

Cracks in the Ice

Julya Rabinowich

THE EUROPE WE KNOW TODAY, the Europe of common factors, is still young. Almost as young as the people who have unthinkingly received its wealth of opportunities, laid in their cradles as a gift from the fairies. The old Europe is shifting away, apparently blurring in the shadow of memory, almost disappeared from the consciousness of advancing generations. That world marked out by borders, in some cases insurmountable, laid down in Europe between East and West. Those heavily-guarded, barbed-wire-reinforced borders, in those days, scaled on pain of death. Borders with dramatic escape attempts, with soldiers and earth roiled-up in death strips. Patrols and the hoarse barks of guard dogs. Berlin was the beating heart of this Europe-wide fragmentation, a terrifying and fascinating hybrid of East and West. West Germany and the GDR. Linked by well-guarded cracks between the worlds. Checkpoint Charlie was a spaceport from which to leap into another galaxy. On either side of that border, people were largely clueless about what lay beyond. Crossing the worlds was like leaping into a black hole. The Eastern Bloc ceased to exist at the Iron Curtain. The world had frozen in the held breath of the Cold War, and Vienna was a small, much-visited island between the two. It was during this time that the tides carried my little family to Vienna, where we got caught up like driftwood. And luckily so.

When I was nineteen, this apparently stable state of torpor began to tremble. Bricks loosened from walls and crashed to the ground, falling across decades-old lines drawn to divide the land both on the map and in its real form. Europe as we knew it morphed bit by bit into a new, open, common Europe. Shortly after the Wall fell, I moved to Berlin for a while. The great euphoria, the intoxication of freedom, the creative dialogue along the Wall are experiences forever anchored in my mind – brighter, more intense, uncanny and exciting than almost anything else. And I have not forgotten it my whole life long, that atmosphere of starting anew. With all the unexplored, and yet, common factors.

Back when the first sections of the Wall broke down and contemporary history was written – tangibly, palpably, co-operatively – Europe was not yet where it stood a few years later. What had once split Germany in two was surmounted. Great days lay ahead of us, we thought at the time.

What lay behind us, though? That steel fencing was not the first of its kind.

Europe has donned its barbed-wire dress several times. People prevented from leaving their country died, chased down in hiding places, driven together like animals, degraded, de-humanised, emaciated, skin stretched taut over bones. Children playing in piles of corpses, seeking protection from the wind and weather. That too is our European past. *Never again*, it was said back then, and today we gaze once more into the hideous face of this de-humanisation, born again, albeit not derailing at full speed. Not yet. Our common Europe is thus the response to the destruction wrought by the Holocaust upon the European body. It is intended to place our common factors over those that divide us. It is intended to tear down borders of the mind and our territories. It is intended to unite and enable common growth. It is intended as the opposite of what once was. The idea is beautiful. But also, a little delusory. The ice of civilisation is thin, too thin to carry out test drillings of a political nature. The ice is thin and its cracking is clearly audible in times like these.

The ability for empathy is what might help humankind survive. This aggression and waning of empathy, incidentally, are the deadly sins that Stephen Hawking regards as a threat to humankind's survival as a species. What can be done when inhibition levels fall while sea levels rise? Unfamiliar tides await us. The safety and security to which we are so accustomed – they are not guaranteed. They are a mere promise that might perhaps no longer be kept if the fronts become entrenched. We only have this one world, and at the moment, Hawking's recommendation to resettle in space is unachievable science fiction.

The waters are rising. The inhibition levels, however, are falling.

Stephen Hawking was a scientist of great genius, whose theories were well-founded. I am merely one writer among many. And yet I want to believe in a better world and a better outcome. I want to believe in humankind. And in its ability to develop further. I want to believe that we might not develop only weapons capable of bringing us death and extinction a hundred times over. We can also develop a way of cooperating, a culture of dialogue that might secure a different future for us.

And now, Europe? What once was divided is now expected to grow. Another thing growing, however, is the resistance against uniting. And nationalism is on the rise too. The nationalism that the European Union set out to end, and likewise the nationalism whose political representatives have often developed a remarkable closeness to Russia, particularly to Vladimir Putin. Presumably not without reason, when we keep finding leaks about monetary transfers from Russia to parties like Marine Le Pen's, for instance.

What might help repair this rupture? What might put a stop to this fragmentation?

We need a Europe of affinity. A Europe of empathy. A Europe of cooperation and equal opportunity. Only with firm ground beneath our feet can we reach for the stars – including those set against a blue background. We need a Europe of self-confidence. Of moral conviction. And that's where the next question arises. The much-touted European values – what exactly are they? Worshipping the past while disregarding its crimes? Or recalling what makes humans human: compassion and responsibility? Recalling what makes Europeans European: the Enlightenment and humanism? And if that's the case, how do we now deal with the deaths in the Mediterranean? The lifeless corpses of children floating on the water of our next beach holiday – do we suppress the thought of them, do we prevent them?

How does Europe explain this failure on its borders? How do we explain the reception camps in Greece, the starving refugees in Hungary, where the state refuses to provide them with food so as to encourage them to leave the country? How can the European Union watch Viktor Orbán's actions, the destruction of press freedom, the unleashing of darkest instincts – right-wing populists always resort to the darkest of instincts, a simple, effective and cheap solution that will cost us all dearly.

I am writing this piece in Vienna, the city that was always poised between East and West, a Checkpoint Charlie of a different kind, a political fulcrum in the style of *The Third Man* and a neutral site of the United Nations. But also a country that has veiled its complicity in the Holocaust, unlike Germany – Austria with its myth of being Hitler's first victim – and at the same time a country that has made great contributions in the humanitarian sector, the country that gave me a new home and that I regard as my country, the country which I therefore demand does the right thing more firmly than I demand of other places not as dear to my heart. I love the narrow, winding streets around St Stephen's Cathedral, I love the magnificent buildings along the Ring, the rustic taverns selling local wine, the cool museum quarter, the range of culture on offer, the literature and the biting wit, and I love the safety and security it still provides. And yet: as I sit at my desk and look out of my window, I see Stumbling Stones, the brass cobblestones inscribed with the names of the Jews murdered after 1938, remembrance cast in metal outside the front doors of their former abodes. And right next door to me, someone has drawn a swastika in the dusty glass of a flat being renovated. That is the reality of Europe at this moment. That which we believed surmounted has returned. To date, it is erratic, blurred, not yet fully materialised; the sleep of reason is still in the act of producing its monsters.

We want to be a moral instance, an embodiment of *Never again*, we want to be enlightened and humanist? Then we must tackle all these issues. Earnestly. Decisively. There is not much time left to act. Already the structure is swaying, already bricks are falling from facades once thought solid, already the ice is cracking beneath our feet. Listen very closely. You can hear it now, at this moment. We want to be human and remain so? Good. Then let us take action. Now.

Translated from the German by Katy Derbyshire

Staging Europe

Annelies Beck

UMBERTO ECO'S RESPONSE TO my first question was booming laughter. We were sitting in a taxi, cruising along the Rue Royal through Brussels, the capital of Europe. I was a young journalist at the time, working on my first novel (facts alone didn't do the human experience justice, I felt). He was Umberto Eco, the Italian writer and European intellectual. We were making a detour on the way to the airport, allowing me to steal some time for an interview. I had asked him whether he liked Brussels and he had laughed. 'Considering that you live here, politeness requires me to say "Yes, of course". It's not an interesting question.' This was the beginning of our conversation.

It was July 2001. Looking back now it feels like the last innocent summer: 9/11 was still a few months away; Facebook wouldn't start holding our attention hostage for another year or two; and climate change wasn't considered more of a threat than it had been in the '80s and '90s when we all wore T-shirts saying: 'No time to waste'.

I was indeed living in Brussels and that summer, Europe came to town. That is to say, Brussels had been the official capital of the European Union for years already, of course. The EU had landed in Brussels much like a shard of glass lodged in a hand. It was a separate part of the city where buildings with mirrored windows suggested transparency rather than offered it; a beer was more expensive in this quarter, and 'eurocrats' flew in and out every week to earn big paycheques. Reporting on what was going on in the EU was, more often than not, focussed on its institutions rather than on Europeans. In short, not many people living in Brussels, or beyond for that matter, felt the EU pertained to them, in spite of the euro and the cheap labour that it made possible.

But all of that was going to change. Belgium had taken on the six-month rotating presidency of the council of European heads of states for the second half of that year. The idea was to put a *heart* into the European Union, a heart called Brussels. The then Belgian prime minister Guy Verhofstadt – who was big on symbolism and a firm believer in the EU – brought together a group of wise men (and two women) from all over Europe to discuss the best way to mark Brussels as a capital of and, most importantly, *for* all Europeans. (Yes, in 2001 it was still possible to include only two women among those great minds.)

'Could it be a building? A piece of music? A monument?,' the prime minister wondered aloud. It was up to the gathered sages to decide. They discussed the matter over dinner at Erasmus House, the site where Desiderius Erasmus – a humanist and the prototypical European intellectual – stayed for a few months in 1521, writing letters, enjoying the beautiful garden and discussing the state of the world with his friends. One of the participants in the 21st-century version of this exchange of ideas was Umberto Eco, the man I shared a taxi with at the end of that day. It hadn't been made clear yet what the result was of all the brainstorming and wining and dining at Erasmus House. (And as it turned out, it never would be.) Eco, however, had a personal view he didn't mind sharing.

'A true city is like a theatre. It offers wide perspectives

with a finely calculated distribution of grand monuments. You have to be careful: throw around too many imposing buildings and they lose grace, think of what the Nazis did.' We were still driving along the Rue Royal with the Palais de Justice looming ahead of us, a giant building with a golden-tinged dome, shrouded in scaffolding for decades, in a perpetual state of salvage from ruin, as opposed to restoration or improvement. Needless to say, the metaphor wasn't lost on Eco.

'It is not enough for Brussels, or any city, to have a brilliant artist design a wonderful monument, compose a piece of music or sculpt a statue, for people to relate to it as the capital of the EU.'

We made a stop in the European Quarter and drank a coffee – a proper coffee – on a terrace at the Luxemburg Square, in front of the European Parliament. 'I can only see it working as a hub, a place where every Erasmus student feels obliged, intellectually and morally, to spend at least three months during the course of their studies. A city where the ruling class of tomorrow learn the trade, form bonds with each other and the city.' His eyes lit up. 'And I mean bonding in the most literal sense: marrying each other, learning each other's languages, appreciating each other's food.'

Eco told me stories about his wife, who's German, and about his favourite food. 'In thirty years, Europe will be a colourful continent, not only in terms of skin but in terms of ideas. It will be a continent where all kinds of religions will have to live together. To learn to appreciate each other's culinary traditions is a fundamental way to learn about one another's mentality!'

It was an exciting idea: Brussels as both the pole of attraction and the springboard for the next generation, the first truly European generation, from Warsaw to London, from Stockholm to Madrid, whether they'd be the ones manning the institutions, artistically shaping European reality or exchanging recipes and vegetables, grown back home. His vision appealed to me, being of the interrail generation myself and having studied abroad: I could imagine this whirl of like-minded young potentials all too well. But could it ever work for everyone?

It was time for Eco to catch that plane, and he did.

Today there's no way you could risk a detour through Brussels' city centre in a taxi (or even an Uber) on the way to the airport. Twenty years on, cars are losing the fight for public space to pedestrians, electrical bikes and public transport, but until the battle is truly over, people pay in time, health and nerves. The Palais de Justice is still standing, held up by scaffolding. In the European Quarter, more glass buildings have arisen, adding to the labyrinthine aspect of that part of the city, with the fissures of the financial crisis of 2008 plastered over. The terrorist attacks in 2016 laid bare other tears in the city's fabric. Brussels has changed and so has Europe.

I wonder what Umberto Eco would make of Europe today – he died in February 2016. No doubt his ideas of 2001 about enlightened and truly European bureaucrats and politicians are deemed elitist by some. His understanding of the need for recognition of local and historical traditions would be considered provincial by others.

Whereas back then the shape and future of Europe seemed to have been the prerogative of politicians and intellectuals having a civil conversation, the question today is of a much more pressing nature than the role of 'Brussels'. The conversation has turned into a shouting match between parties calling each other names ('elites', 'nationalists', 'cosmopolitans', etc.) and, more importantly, challenging the role of the European Union. The EU is too much or too little, too loud or too quiet, too unified or too divided.

Men continue to pontificate, sometimes wisely too. But,

thankfully, more and more women now raise their voices and make themselves heard. Eco was right: bonds are being forged across boundaries. 'Climate kids' take to the streets, inspired by a Swedish girl, and hold the EU to account for what it is failing to do. Young men from Hungary to Belgium calling themselves '*identitaires*' challenge the idea of the EU altogether. The debate is no longer about symbols or a shared capital. The next generation is talking about survival, recognition, dignity, and home, albeit in many different and often contradictory ways.

Whether it is being rejected as the root of all evil or embraced as the start of the solution, the EU is finally, and somewhat ironically, at the heart of the debate. On second thought, 'debate' may be too civilised a word for the clash that is being fought on so many different fronts: on the streets and social media more so than in political arenas. Politics has become a spectacle, a theatrical event with effect trumping essence. It quickens the blood and raises the stakes in equal measure. The 'inner emigration' of Europeans who don't feel at home anymore in their own country and who, as Hannah Arendt put it, withdraw to an interior realm, into the 'invisibility of thinking and feeling,' is as much part of what threatens to break up the European construction as the perceived threat of actual people crossing the Mediterranean. Migration is not only a movement of people but also of minds. Citizens hesitate between wearily shaking their head or turning their backs on it all.

But a story *is* being written and it will play itself out far beyond the theatre that is Brussels. Some scripts are being prompted from the wings across the ocean, whispering the catchphrase 'Take Back Control'. Others are being tested in citizens' panels or forums that are redesigning democracy with an eye on the future. Every European, old and new, here or on the way, has a stake in this story – stories, plural. There are many, many sides to the debate. Eco's 'wide perspectives' are ever more fractured, much like a kaleidoscope wherein fragments constantly realign themselves in unimaginable patterns.

So how to bond and bridge all those elements, all those people in their multifaceted individuality? How to leave room to manoeuvre and at the same time hold the continent together? Is it possible to blend and at the same time respect the where, whence and how of the parts that make up the whole? Brexit taught us that breaking away comes at a cost. Since the last European elections, it looks like fewer parties want out, but more – and perhaps louder ones – want it done differently.

A foundation of facts won't suffice to hold up the European project. An empty theatre, no matter how grand it looks, is a soulless place. There's not just the one story that should hijack the stage and occupy the theatre. There should be room for more. Stories can work in a myriad of ways; they are not in themselves good or bad. But they can unlock hearts and minds and lay bare the shared humanity of all, more so than newly invented symbols. They can put a wedge in shrill sounding certainties that are sold as unassailable truths.

I'm still a journalist, trying to gain footing in fact. But I'm ever more the novelist, examining the more complicated ways in which we exist. My first question to Eco, 'Do you like Brussels?', wasn't an interesting one – he was right. There are other questions to be asked: 'What do you think of…?, How do you feel about… ?', 'Who are you…?, What is your life like… ?', 'What do you suggest…?' Questions that set off stories. The power of a story lies in a voice speaking up. The power of a story lies in its multiplicity. The power of every story lies in it being listened to.

Two Lakes

Kapka Kassabova

Dedicated to the people of the Balkans

THE TOPOGRAPHIC FEATURES OF the mountain had telling names, in no chronological order. Here was, simply, a treasurescape of centuries: Coffin-Maker, Wolf's Lair, Bloodied Stone, Lost Souls, Mean Valley, and beyond the shadowy side of Mean Valley was Albania. Not that anything had been *simple* here, where even the name of this country was recently altered with a geographical signifier, to 'North Macedonia'. In fact, we were in the far south of the western Balkans.

My guide Angelo and I were climbing the sunny side of the valley. The opposite flank was topped by the rusty antennae of a Cold War-era observation station. For fifty years, the Albanian and the Yugoslav sides spied on each other over Mean Valley, on this once-impermeable border. The people of the lakes could see each other across the water they have shared since pre-history, yet for half a century of Cold War, this border kept them in parallel realities. Those who attempted to cross were shot, even children. Today, once you pass the sleepy Saint Naum checkpoint by the lakeside and walk into Albanian territory among birdsong and cherry trees, all you see from that era are the bunkers.

While we puffed up the path marked by brown bear dung, the mountain felt like a barrier between the lakes. As with a border, you were either on one side or the other, your view limited to one lake. The other lurked somewhere beyond, unknown, vast, disquieting with its otherness. Although the lakes are five kilometres apart as the pelican flies, it takes an hour to drive across them, along a switchback road built by political prisoners in the first decade of Tito's regime.

Now, two thousand metres above sea-level, a new perspective opened. To the west was Lake Ohrid, a giant blue crater – no wonder its early name was Lychnitis, lake of light. To the east was the higher Lake Prespa, meaning 'snow drift', with its cold undertones. Ohrid is a perfect oval. Prespa is a jagged tear shape. The limestone shores of the Lakes are full of medieval cave churches and niches painted with frescoes so life-like they almost walk off the walls towards you. Prespa also has a companion 'mini-me' lakelet, Mikri Prespa, but they were separated by a post-WWI border: the mother lake is split among (North) Macedonia, Albania, and Greece; the little one is in Greece but with its tail end in Albania. From up here, you could survey the insanity of treating these ancient lakes and mountains like nothing more than a geopolitical pie, though the national borders were invisible to the naked eye. You had to know they were there. Locals, including fishermen, were prohibited from crossing into neighbouring lake territory, and they knew exactly where in the water the invisible lines ran and when to turn the boat back towards land. Although you could hear the Italian music of Albanian fish restaurants while having lunch on the Macedonian side, you could not just swim there, or take a boat – you had to use the official checkpoint.

'Now do you see?' Angelo beamed. Despite his disfigured back, the result of a paragliding accident, he didn't get out of breath. 'The lakes and the mountains are a complete ecological and spiritual system.'

The mountain ranges unfolded all the way to the Aegean in the south and the Adriatic to the west, uninterrupted. The two lakes are connected through underground rivers that run under the mountain: Prespa above fed Ohrid below and by the time the water reached the lower lake, it was filtered by the karstic mountain, making it Europe's largest natural body of clean water, as well as Europe's oldest lake, and the only lacustrine biosphere of this kind in Eurasia. Mikri Prespa has the world's largest nesting colony of Dalmatian pelicans; they overwinter in Africa and make their spectacular return in May, except for the older individuals who stay home all year.

'See the craters?' Angelo pointed at the pockmarked hillside below. The Macedonian Front had passed through here – the most strategic Balkan front during the First World War and the site of tens of thousands of multi-national deaths. The craters came from mortar explosions, and there were remains of trenches, hacked into the stone by the Bulgarian army with Sysiphean devotion. The French Oriental Army shelled them across Mean Valley, in snow and sunshine, with numberless Cameroonians and Senegalese dying of exposure, leaving gold napoleons buried under stones – or so the locals believed. A generation later, the Italian front in Albania stretched to the west.

Heaven and hell met above the Lakes. The Earth gave us heaven, we provided the hell. Seen from the plateau, the Lakes were like eyes in an ancient face. Each generation had sacrificed its children, as in a Greek tragedy, to appease some perverse god. There had been winning sides, but no winners.

'These border mountains with Greece are full of human bones,' Angelo said.

On the far side of Lake Prespa was a checkpoint with Greece, closed during that country's military dictatorship.

For half a century, the people on each side have been banned from walking down the lakeside road into the first village on the other side where they have relatives. Instead, they must spend half a day crossing mountainous hinterlands, passing through a remote checkpoint, travelling one hundred and seventy kilometres to return to this same lakeside. Only bears and wolves roam free. I made this journey too – you end up a couple of miles up shore from where you started, but only after much time, expense, and driving eerie mountain roads haunted by the ruined villages of the Greek Civil War. This journey of the severed lake-checkpoint was symbolic of the zero-sum achievement of hard borders. And what are hard borders but the manifestation of a state of siege?

'And over there,' he pointed towards the ancient town of Ohrid at the northern tip of the lake, where my maternal grandmother was from, 'passed the Via Egnatia.'

The Roman trade route that traversed the southern Balkans from Durres to Istanbul brought trade, invaders, and crusaders from the West, and trade, invaders, and Christian and Muslim mystics from the East, all the way from Persia. Thanks to the Egnatian road and geopolitical forces in far-off imperial capitals, the Lakes had known prosperity and peace, war and destitution, and in the last hundred years – mass emigration. Above the lake stood ghostly houses, like old people wanting to tell you something before they die.

'There's just a few of us left,' Angelo said. 'Like the old pelicans in winter.'

He was from a village on Lake Ohrid, once part of the estate of the Monastery of Saint Naum, named after the ninth-century monk who healed the insane, and where my great-grandmother liked to go – for the fine beach sand which cleaned her kitchen pots like nothing else, she said. But the lakes' people kept leaving, generation after generation, as my grandmother had done. Angelo was 'trying not to emigrate' because he loved his homeland. I loved it here too. I had come to the Lakes to seek answers to a question as much personal as collective because the local is inseparable from the global: how to move forwards instead of backwards into the abyss?

We rummaged inside the disused Yugoslav military barracks by the observation station on the plateau, although it had been thoroughly plundered since its decommissioning. Angelo had seen men carry fridges and ovens on their backs over Mean Valley. We found cans from the 1950s, stamped 'Yugoslavia', and empty cartridge shells from the 1980s. The mountain, like the Lakes, kept churning up memories.

But before we turned into history's scavengers, something strange happened. I picked an alpine flower, instantly regretting it – you should never pick alpine flowers – and Angelo exploded as if it had been a grenade. I had no right to pick that flower, this wasn't my mountain. Things escalated. There were national insults because we were of different nationalities, though our ancestors weren't. We were dazed with sunshine and altitude, but it was also the nature of this mountain to confront us. Its memories of a siege had invaded our minds. I stepped back and nearly fell into a trench – into the war graves of a hundred years ago.

Angelo's and my great-grandfather had fought in that war, on the same side, the losing side. His great-grandfather had deserted; mine had emigrated. Our grandfathers had fought in the next war. Angelo and I, in turn, were children of the Cold War. Our families were scattered across the world through waves of emigration. As a young man, he had taken part in the brief and nasty conflict that had spilt over from Kosovo into (North) Macedonia. And here we were, after all of that, ready to rip out each other's throats over a flower. The collective narrative of suffering and siege had infected our personal identity. We could not let go of the suffering – *our* suffering which was not, in fact, ours; it belonged to this whole peninsula, this whole continent. In the circular executioner-victim narrative that chases its tail like a rabid dog, we were always the victims, of course. The shadow was on the other side of Mean Valley, not with us. This cognitive dissonance has caused the peoples of the Balkans to endlessly divide, checkpoint after closed checkpoint, siege after senseless siege, destroying the peace of generations. And like the child presented to Solomon, dividing amounted to killing – either immediately, or later. This is why we all carry the wounds of Balkanisation, and here we were, acting them out again. Trauma demands repetition, the child psychiatrist Selma Freiberg wrote – until it is made conscious and healed. And in his seminal essay 'The Uncanny', Sigmund Freud said: 'The archaic heritage of human beings comprises not only dispositions but also subject matter – memory-traces of the experience of earlier generations.'

The biosphere of the Lakes with their borders running against nature, as well as against humanity, is a microcosm of the Balkans. And the Balkans are a confluence of the West which came late and the East which never went away. Whatever happens in the Balkans will manifest elsewhere, and that which is happening in Europe today has already taken place in the Balkans not long ago. Mid-crisis, Angelo and I stopped insulting each other and became rooted to the spot on the plateau, with the wind throwing our words away – and we saw what we were doing. We were ghosts shouting in our predecessors' voices, out of compulsive loyalty. We carried their suffering like the scavengers carrying fridges on their backs. And in doing this, we were robbing ourselves of the present moment rich with sublime nature, summer and friendship. Who has a future? Those who don't get caught up in war, again. Those who hear the urgent message of the past.

War incubates within and spreads without. It can be

dormant for a generation, then stoked by the intent of hate which begins with language and catches like influenza. War begins with division – us and them – which is a form of inequality.

We made our descent towards the Lake of Light, having made our peace, words having run out. The shadow moved over Mean Valley. Albania's mountains, gilded with sunset, looked mythical. Above Lake Ohrid, Alexander the Great had arguably fought his most destructive Balkan campaign, against an Illyrian city, before setting out east. The modern Greeks and (North) Macedonians have spent a quarter-century arguing over who owns that man, thus perpetuating his antique war while the future remained closed, like the checkpoint on Prespa.

One hundred years after the border went up, in 2019, Prespans were heartened by news that the disused checkpoint was finally going to be re-opened, after the Prespa Agreement between the two countries, a de facto peace agreement. The erased road on the Greek side would be rebuilt. The handsome empty villages on both sides would have visitors, children might return, cousins meet again. It wouldn't take much – only the right intent. It wouldn't take much for lakes where you can swim without a passport, where you can go from one town to the next without being shot or made to climb mountains in some Sysiphean punishment for a sin long forgotten but not forgiven – a sin committed by the forefathers, yet we are left with the bill. Cronos loves to devour his children, though he will deny it, citing historic grievances instead. We must call his bluff and walk away from the war trenches.

Is that too much to wish for, or too little? It is exactly right. The Ohrid-Prespa Lakes are between one and three million years old. Humans have only lived in Europe for 46,000 years. How long is a human life? Not long, though a siege can be endless.

A lake is the opposite of a border. When you look at a barbed fence, you think of death. When you look at a lake, you remember that we come from water, return to water, and without water, we shrivel up – and then you think of eternity and want to make amends before it's too late.

In Human Form

Asja Bakić

'Look,' said H.H. 'That there below us is Europa. What a beauty!'

I tried to make out the bull with a girl on its back, but from that height, it still wasn't possible to see animals.

'I can't see her,' I said. 'Could you point her out? Her picture isn't in the document you gave me.'

'I don't mean the person,' said H.H. 'I'm talking about the European continent.'

I didn't know what continents looked like. I'd assumed they were larger, but Europe looked tiny, human-sized, as if it really could have been a person.

'It looks… fragile,' I said.

'Everything on Earth is like that,' noted H.H. 'That's why we've come here, for you to learn.'

They told me I would live for one human lifetime.

'That's an instant, less than an instant,' I said. 'How can I learn enough about people, about ourselves, in such a short time?'

'That's not important now,' they said.

H.H. proposed I choose a book to occupy myself with while I was alive.

'Or perhaps even just one sentence,' he said. 'One sentence

for a lifetime, that's quite enough.'

I didn't know what a book was, or a lifetime for that matter. Or Europe even. The unfamiliar language H.H. was using seemed terribly difficult. I was convinced I'd never master it.

'Keep track of everything you collect. We'll contact you periodically with tips. Good luck!'

With those words, they placed me in a human body. I lived in Europe and Europe lived in me. How this worked wasn't clear to me, but I kept my distance from bulls. I knew that mammals couldn't walk on water. With each passing day, I understood less. Why was the entire continent named after a kidnapped girl? And why had they sent me here, of all places? Learning new things usually came easily to me, but human nature continued to elude me. I often wondered if I was unable to grasp it because Europe had such a narrow view of the rest of the world – or was Europe so singularly complex that I had no time to concern myself with other things? Contemplating Europe gave me my first headache.

'That's not surprising,' read H.H.'s message. 'Europeans sometimes strain to understand. They strain while doing some other things, too, but we won't discuss that now.'

The years passed faster than I'd first imagined. About ten days before my death, when they were finally supposed to come for me, a fear I'd never experienced before began to grip me. I awaited their return with trepidation.

'When we call you,' H.H. said, 'you'll know exactly where to go. Don't bring anything but your notebook. And give some thought to the title.'

'All right,' I said.

When he'd contacted me the first time, H.H. hadn't held back any detail of what it meant to be a person, painstakingly describing the processes I would go through. Now, all of a sudden, I began to notice my face. And as the end of my time as a human drew nearer, my excitement over physiognomy grew too. Ultimately that excitement turned to sorrow over the fact that a human could exist and cease to exist so quickly. At the same time, I was masturbating more because H.H.'s descriptions brought the human body, which I'd never previously considered, closer to me. I often found myself ruminating on rumination. Everything was connected.

'Thinking, for example,' he once said, 'can be as pleasurable as masturbation.'

'Really?' I asked, remembering my headache.

'I believe so, but the human body is an enigma and we'll never be entirely sure,' he replied.

H.H. smiled, so I smiled in turn, but the edge of my lip quivered as if my thoughts were pulling me in the other direction. It was a sad smile. If I'd understood correctly, sadness was a distinctly European feeling that could vary in its intensity, but those nuances eluded me no matter how much H.H. tried to make them clearer.

'How long have you known I'd end up here?' I asked.

'From the beginning,' said H.H. 'That's the procedure.'

'Why didn't you tell me right away? I could've prepared better.'

'You would never have been ready for Europe,' said H.H.

I'd spent my whole human life compulsively taking notes and now I was poring over them. H.H. asked me to put a name to my experience, but I didn't know how best to encapsulate it. *European Life*? It sounded too vague, but it wasn't: I'd lived in Europe and that was no small thing. At one point in the notebook, I wrote the word 'European' followed by a question mark. I wanted to find out, before my time was up, what that word actually meant. H.H. repeated a hundred times that not all people were the same, that people differed from each other even when they lived on the same continent, though in the end it hardly mattered.

'That difference sounds like a lie,' I said.

'Why?' H.H. asked.

'Well, given that the human body always maintains the life it holds in the same way, one body can't be different from another. All people are the same.'

'Do you think you're the same?'

'I'm not a person,' I said.

There was this author Novalis, I once wrote down, who'd claimed that the human form can contain beings completely different from people. It dawned on me while reading these notes that I should give my diary the title *In Human Form* because I was that completely different being. It seemed to me that Europeans were different beings too. We had a lot in common: we regarded human suffering from a respectable distance, with curiosity. We learned, but laboriously.

When H.H. and I discussed what made a person – what made me a person, even though I wasn't one – we arrived at the same conclusion: that I would die. In our world there was no such finality; this was the main difference between us and humans. On Earth, there were plants that could travel through time by way of their seeds, which would hibernate, waiting for an opportune moment to sprout. Plants could anticipate a dry year and simply skip it, but people couldn't time-travel – they couldn't suspend time. I asked, of course, why they'd thrown me like a seed onto European soil. H.H. claimed I would figure it out soon enough.

'Some things we'll explain to you afterwards,' he said.

'I would love,' I said, a bit absently, 'for something of what I've written to remain.'

'That wouldn't be in accordance with the rules,' H.H. said.

'You need to destroy everything?' I asked.

'For the death to be complete, your words need to die with you.'

'That's ridiculous,' I said. 'Words aren't people – they can't die.'

'So you want us to keep your notes, but kill all the people who could read them?'

I didn't like where the conversation was heading; for the first time, I realised that my stay in Europe had been too brief and that I hadn't really learnt anything. On top of that, they'd asked me to die without leaving any tangible traces, any evidence that I'd existed as a person.

'Do you understand now what a European is?'

'Nobody and nothing?'

'Exactly,' H.H. confirmed. 'Nobody and nothing.'

Before I finished my last diary entry, H.H. called me and said we needed to find the place previously known as the Socialist Federal Republic of Yugoslavia. Pronouncing that name gave me trouble – I stumbled over the words.

'It's fairly close. The compass will help you.'

I briefly considered not responding to the call, not going. My justification would be: 'I don't understand the name of the place.'

I thought they'd deliberately chosen the Socialist Federal Republic of Yugoslavia because it was a tongue-twister and no longer existed. They wanted me to see how everything disappeared on Earth, everything changed, especially those things people insisted were eternal.

'Tuberculosis,' I read aloud.

The disease was mentioned in a footnote on Europe. The next digital note summarised SFRY in a few sentences, and the compass began blinking when I set foot on the terrain that no longer bore this name. I waited a few moments, then H.H. appeared in front of me.

'Is it time for me to finally sprout?' I asked.

H.H. smiled; he loved metaphors. He recognised the European spirit in them.

'Give me your notebook.' He held out his hand. 'What did you call it?'

'*In Human Form*,' I said.

'You chose well,' he said, setting fire to the notebook. 'Only your body is left now.'

He said this as if it were easier to burn me than the diary.

'Why did I need to name something you didn't even bother opening?' I asked.

'It's harder to detach ourselves from the things we name,' said H.H.

'Then why don't I have a name?'

'Because then it would be even harder to detach yourself from your life, and that's not the point of this exercise.'

'It's vulgar to call human life an exercise.'

'Perhaps, but you're not human. Why should you care?'

I'd spent just one lifetime in human form. I wasn't supposed to care.

'I don't know,' I said.

Maybe, as a European, I found it especially difficult to adapt to change?

'According to the rules, in human skin you should feel emotions we can't, you should feel a loneliness that doesn't exist for us, and, most importantly, you should die in order to appreciate your own immortality.'

'Well, this was a failed exercise then, because there are some emotions I never had time to feel.'

I watched as H.H.'s two halves both cocked their heads. We were double beings, never alone – the idea of loneliness was completely foreign to us since we perceived everything as a duo. We could understand the death of the individual better than people could, if we had to.

'When I die, what then?' I asked.

'Your name and the same old perspective you're used to will return to you.'

But what had that perspective been like? I couldn't recall. For years I'd been a European, nobody and nothing, and now I could only think like one.

'What will become of Europe?'

I wanted to know. I was on the verge of shouting: 'Give me another lifetime! I don't know anything!'

The thought that next time they might send me to some other continent filled me with dread. Europe was the centre of my world.

'Time's up,' H.H. said abruptly.

He hadn't answered my question. He rubbed his hands together like he'd finished some kind of lucrative assignment. Flames erupted under my feet. As time receded, my doubleness slowly returned. Europe was fading from my sight.

'A beauty indeed,' I thought.

In the place where Europe had been, there remained a tiny emptiness. The other continents and the celestial bodies were too big to fill the void.

'I'll miss it,' I said softly.

I wanted to kidnap the whole continent and take it with me into the future.

It was as if H.H. could read my mind.

'You can't kidnap a kidnapper,' he said.

I couldn't understand what he meant by this. My double swayed back and forth as if I were riding the flame that engulfed me. I no longer had legs, but that didn't matter.

Translated from the Croatian by Jennifer Zoble

Hummingbird

Nora Nadjarian

Preface

The first hummingbird lived in Europe over 30 million years ago. Its colours were bright and bold, magnificent and stirring. When the hummingbird hovered above a flower with that spectacular blur of wings, its heartbeat was unbelievable.

This is a beginning.

1. The Necessity of Smiling

The woman pulls aside the bed covers and touches her belly. She's getting heavier around the waist but her husband still looks at her with desire, she thinks. After a long day's work, as he lies in bed exhausted, he sometimes strokes her absent-mindedly while thinking about his next paycheque, about the bills or rent. He doesn't tell her about their troubles.

Every now and then, at night, he feels the urge to enter his pregnant wife. He is careful not to press her belly too hard, not to break anything. His wife is filling up with strange liquids, with milk, with fat. And things can break, he has heard. Even water.

Lately, she reminds him of a woman in an old black and white photograph he once found tucked inside the last page of his father's passport, a few days after he'd died. A large, wide-hipped woman lying on a bed of crumpled sheets, smiling. Her long hair covered her full breasts. Part of the bedsheet covered her sex. He remembers the desire he'd felt looking at his father's mistress, mixed with the pain of losing him. The woman had been part of his father's secret past. After looking at it for a long time, he had destroyed the photograph and handed the passport to his grieving mother.

When they first arrived here, he and his wife had a short conversation about smiling.

'Should we smile at our neighbours?'

'I think we should. We don't speak the same language.'

'But is it necessary to smile?'

'Yes.'

'And if you feel like crying?'

'Hide your tears.'

Babies are born crying, bawling for whatever it is they seem to have lost, whatever it is they seem to have found – yet the whole world welcomes them with a smile. This was not the case with the son of the immigrants. He came into the world prematurely, without so much as a whimper. With a pink face and a shock of black hair, he looked wisely, defiantly, at his first surroundings, his first, blurred, world – but did not cry.

2. A Game

There are three loud knocks on the door in the middle of the night and the old man wakes up with a start and thinks it's the police. That is the first thing that comes to mind. He can hardly see a thing. This is ridiculous, he thinks. What's going on? He turns on the bedside lamp. It's 2 a.m. He drags himself out of bed, puts on his slippers and squints all the way to the front door, which he has locked from the inside. He unlocks the door and finds that funny-looking boy from next door standing before him on the porch – the boy with the imp-like body and the face of a wise man.

'We've found her,' the boy says. 'We've found Irini.'

'Irini? Who's Irini?'

'Peace.'

'You've found Peace?'

In Greek, there is no distinction. Irini means Peace, Peace means Irini.

The old man should feel angry at having been woken up for nothing, but he feels more tired than anything. He feels more tired than he's ever felt in his life. This must be some kind of a joke. Nobody has ever found Peace, he thinks, especially on this island. He wonders if it's all a dream. The boy must be playing games with him and he wants to slam the door in his face. Maybe it was a bet with a friend: 'Go and wake up some fools in your neighbourhood in the middle of the night and tell them you've found Peace. If they believe you, I'll give you 10 Euros.' It was a bet and the boy had lost.

The unwanted visitor runs away and leaves the old man empty-handed and blue, the blue of disappointment. Irini lets out a long laugh.

She is what eludes us, what slips away from us. It occurs to the old man that he's waited a lifetime for peace. He's disappointed that she has never, ever appeared to him, not even in a dream. The future, ah. The future, ah. 'Ah' is the word Cypriots use when there is no real answer or they can't think of anything else to say. Ah, we're out of sausages. Ah, the bank was shut. Ah, the peace talks have fallen through. Ah.

He wants to ask the boy what Irini looks like, but the boy is no longer there. The old man stands bewildered at his door. Ah.

Irini laughs.

3. A Chance Encounter

The woman never loses the weight she put on carrying her son, and he grows up. He speaks many languages, he travels the world. The boy who once spoke in riddles will be a man in no time.

One day, years later, he walks into an Armenian grocery in Vienna or Berlin or Paris or London or around the corner of a very cosmopolitan, beautifully tree-lined, avenue. In this shop, there are things of which his soul is made.

It is a chance encounter. He walks into the shop for no real reason except to take it all in, what is already inside him. All the familiarity of the food which to others may have no meaning at all beyond what it is, but which to him means the world: soujouk, pastourma, apricots, walnuts. A palette of colours, dried fruit displayed in sacks around the shop, sausages coiled inside their packets, bottled smells, dusty tins on high shelves. Perhaps this shop, perhaps this man with his warm, dark eyes, perhaps that bottle of brandy will assure him that a makeshift home is possible, even here, in this exotic, familiar, alien territory, where they sell comfort food in disguise.

It has snowed in this city, and it is, to his eyes, the purest white that white can be, the coldest purity, and the lights of the passing vehicles are piercing. His feet are cold.

'You remind me of someone,' he says. 'This shop reminds me of my childhood. How long have you lived here?'

'Twenty-five years,' says the shopkeeper, who could almost be his father. 'I've lived here for twenty-five years,' in that language of his heart.

They always keep count, those who are away. Three months. Ten weeks. Twenty-five years. Does it matter? One day it will be a million years, but does it really matter as long as you are here? What difference does it make to anyone, that you drink brandy here and not there, that your children speak German or French or English, here and not there?

'We must love the present, not live in the past!' sighs the shopkeeper.

'Oh, but time is a womb,' says the man who speaks in riddles. 'Aren't past and present and future all one?'

The shopkeeper reflects on this. He goes home and asks his daughter: 'What is the future?' His daughter looks up from the textbook she is studying, and replies: 'Whatever you make it.' The man likes that answer and drinks a toast to it with a glass of Armenian brandy, the good stuff, the one he saves for special occasions, for that special drunkenness of his soul.

But tonight he does something he's never done before. He goes out and rings on his neighbours' doorbell. He hears shuffling, a short, muffled conversation behind the wall, and then the door opens. A surprised face greets him.

'Please,' says the shopkeeper, smiling. He wants to share the half-empty bottle of brandy with his blue-eyed neighbour. 'Yes?' he asks, but it is more of an invitation than a question.

With the lamplight shining through it, the brandy takes on the colour of honey.

4. Scattered Ashes

Sometimes, on cosmopolitan, tree-lined avenues, there are violent demonstrations, smashed-in cars and shop windows, tear gas. People hold up banners that bleed words onto the streets. They start running in all directions, without knowing exactly where or why. There are loud knocks on doors, the wails of sirens.

In another part of the city, somebody followed an invisible line which both divided and united. Somebody tried to cross over to the other side – whichever side you happened to be on – and was shot. A woman was arrested. The young anarchist with the beard long enough to sweep the floor said that he wanted to have his ashes scattered over there, beyond the checkpoint, across the border, when he died. They all scoffed at this unthinkable idea. That depends on which way the wind blows. Somebody else said a whole family had drowned when they fell overboard. Not being able to save them had felt like not being able to speak. Whole conversations were lost.

And suddenly there is a deluge of tears and waters breaking and blood and snow and ice melting. Something terrible is happening, and at the same time, it feels as if all this is already in the past.

5. Hovering

The hummingbird returns to its origins after millions of years. It returns in a flash, sips on honey and hope, and glimmers. Its miniature heart beats and beats: I exist, I exist. Its tiny body belies this immense performance. The onlooker, if there is one, feels ashamed, unable to fathom the strenuous act. Everything is hovering and waiting. This hum is how it is, how things are.

A child prodigy once saw a blur of colour and understood its meaning. He went through life making small changes to the way he looked at things. And he claimed to have seen Peace. His parents had no idea what he meant.

Irini smiled.

Europe Must be for the 99 Per Cent

Apolena Rychlíková

IT WAS SIX YEARS AGO, when I brought my older daughter into this world, that fear for the future struck me for the first time. In my arms I held a tiny, beautiful and defenceless creature, taking her first deep breath in a world that was suddenly no longer 'just mine'. Faced with this new life, I suddenly became aware of my own mortality. That sense was accompanied by a question that kept resounding in my head: what kind of world will I, and indeed all of us, leave here for our children. Back then the problems facing our planet were being discussed only in certain circles, and even there only rarely and timidly. They seemed distant and unreal. Now that the countdown to impending ecological doom has begun, the question has been gaining ever greater urgency. And Europe, its transformation, self-reflection and further development, plays a key role in every aspect of this.

The Czech Republic joined the European Union on 1 May 2004. Over 50 per cent of the country's population took part in the referendum, with no less than 70 per cent of them voting *for* accession. However, after fifteen years of EU-citizenship, there is growing mistrust in the entire project. There has been a lot of talk lately about the failure of the post-communist world to transform itself into a classic Western democracy. But what exactly is meant by this?

There is no post-material without the material

The values that trickled into Eastern Europe after the disintegration of the bipolar world of the Cold War-era seem to have got bogged down in a post-material vacuum. The idea that a new, sudden and generally 'democratic' organisation of society would be sufficient to make people change – in tandem with the antagonistic and anti-communist rejection of everything 'social' – became the decisive narrative for building a different Eastern Europe. Back then, people believed that the advent of a generation 'uncorrupted by communism' would bring about a democratic boom for all. That everything would soon be wonderful. It was only a matter of waiting a few years and the transformation of a totalitarian society into a free one would be accomplished. But, as the saying goes, the baby was thrown out with the bathwater. We were so eager to be like the West that we failed to see the problems that the West was grappling with.

The fall of the iron curtain has thus reinforced the triumph of the global politics of ruthless individualism, becoming a dominant political force throughout Europe: the ideals on which former communist societies were built have been discredited forever. And rightly so.

Visionary policies were replaced by unfreedom. However – and this is crucial – nobody was able to come up with a precise definition of the new freedom that dawned in the post-1989 world. Who was it for and how could it be justly distributed? What should be its foundations, and who should profit from it? And should it even bring profit? The East failed to learn from the mistakes that had brought about a gradual fragmentation of society in the West. The starting point of emancipation efforts running across all of post-war Europe –

the longing for a just society (not least specifically in economic terms) – was suddenly out of date. The East reconstituted itself into a class-society and this was really "cool". But the restoration of a class-society has reawakened the spectres that accompanied the start of the dramatic changes in the twentieth century. 'Communism has disappeared, but the problems linked to its origin have not,' said Ludvík Vaculík, one of Czechoslovakia's most important writers, and this is still true today. All we have been left with is extreme capitalism, plain and simple. That is why it is less of a paradox that the social disintegration most of our countries have faced in recent years has grown from similar roots and has even followed a similar course.

While Europe is nowadays divided by a new iron curtain, with the great wage-gap providing the clear and visible dividing line, structural problems within individual nation-states show similar symptoms: growing nationalism, a turn to conservatism, further atomisation of society, and increasingly difficult access to alternatives. We can hardly claim that racism, lack of solidarity, xenophobia and intolerance are something deeply buried in human nature, that these are nothing more than the mindset of a puzzlingly large group of individuals. Rather, an inclination towards undemocratic regimes is, more often than not, the result of a boiling over of long-term frustrations for unfulfilled, even if unarticulated, demands for a dignified and well-rounded life. And when we look at the world today, that is hardly surprising.

Over the course of research into xenophobia and the growth of extreme right-wing views carried out among excluded communities in Germany and France, the main issue respondents would raise sooner rather than later was the declining quality of public services. They spoke about cuts in, or even the scrapping of, public transport routes; about the closed post office that austerity forced to move several kilometres away; about increased rents and the absence of infrastructure in general. Even seemingly trivial things like this can easily make people feel that nobody cares about the common people; that ordinary folk may as well not exist, simply not be there. If someone can't feed their family and pay the rent for a basic flat despite going to work every day, how should this person feel about democracy? And those facing permanent discrimination because of the colour of their skin, how free do they feel? And how is justice perceived by someone who is condemned to poverty by biology – just because she happens to be female?

Although in some respects the divisions between the social certainties of various EU citizens echo the old-world divisions, the two sides reproach each other for almost the same things. While the economically unfulfilled East Europeans suffer from the sense that they are slaving away for the West, the brutally unequal West complains that the East Europeans are taking away its jobs. The dream of a free market and free movement has escalated into a conflict of interest that has begun to break Europe up into a variety of distinct groups. These groups compete with each other while failing to point their finger at the ruling class, let alone threaten it in any effective way that might finally expose the fundamental shortcomings of our Europe – the unequal distribution of property and resources, the inequality of access to public debate, as well as the inequality of responsibility. In a world where inequality is a global problem, where an overwhelming majority of us belong to the weaker 99 per cent of society, this is not just tragic but also absurd.

The Notre Dame is on fire, make a wish

On a recent business trip to France, I visited Marseille. I had only a few hours to stroll around a city I hadn't seen in years. In the middle of a public square, I saw scorched barricades, broken windows and hundreds of people camping out. Outside the university campus, shopping trollies full of bedding had piled up, improvised dwellings that added an unusual touch to the space, blending with it in a way that seemed strangely natural. The people hanging around the park had nowhere to go – they had no home. Housing has become one of today's battlegrounds. As have working conditions. The difference between those who have, or rather, those who 'own', and those who don't have and don't own – but still have to live somewhere and on something – are becoming more and more pronounced. Yet we avert our gaze. How many people in our society freeze to death just because they have nowhere to go? And who is to blame for it? All I had to do was travel a few hundred kilometres to find myself on the Côte d'Azur, watching the sky-blue waves lap against the shore and wonder what this town, so idyllic at first sight, would look like a few years from now. The yachts lining the marina were gently bobbing on the waves. Once climate change hits with full force, the owners and their families will be able to move on and continue to live as before. They have somewhere to go. But what about the others? 'Just move to the country,' I was told by a politician during a mothers' protest against the city authorities' inaction during a period of intense smog. It was almost impossible to go out with children, and pensioners, the sick and other vulnerable groups were just as badly affected. Meanwhile, this politician climbed into the SUV outside his house and drove to his office without a worry in this world, casually fobbing us off with this platitude without realising how inappropriate it was.

One of the problems of the times we live in is that finding the culprits is difficult. It sounds so crass: are we even allowed to ask whose fault it is? But the world is full of conflict, and there are so many of us here, and that is why we shouldn't always seek consensus. A person who can barely meet their basic needs can't be happy just because it's what those who can meet them, easily and many times over, wish. That is partly why a discussion about responsibility ought to be on our mind – if for no other reason than for us to be better able to identify it and be aware of it. And it's not just each individual's responsibility for her- or himself but, first and foremost, for others. For those who haven't been as fortunate in life, who can't flaunt their good education and social, cultural and financial capital. Surely this shouldn't deprive them of the right to a dignified and high-quality life?

In April 2019, as we all gawped, amazed, at the burning Notre Dame Cathedral, few people thought that the flames would expose other things apart from the beams. Soon after the fire broke out, billionaires across Europe offered to open their purses and before we knew it, more than three million euros had been pledged for the cathedral's reconstruction. Where does admiration for such high-mindedness stop at a time when the very same people don't pay taxes in their countries and make no contribution to the building of the networks of solidarity that form the basis of modern society? How are those who feel excluded in today's Europe supposed to respond? Or is, perhaps, this very question sacrilegious, and if so, why? Because we are talking about sacred things, such as a centuries-old cathedral, because the material sphere is still perceived as something cheap.

The desire for a balanced world

Discussions about inequality rarely go beyond the initial statement: oh well, it does exist but that's the world we live in these days. Not everyone can have an equal amount. There's nothing we can do about it. But that's not the point. The crucial discussion concerns something else: how to ensure that the impact of major global problems does not affect only those who cannot defend themselves and, what's more, who don't bear as much responsibility for what is happening to the world. Climate change brings this into a particularly sharp focus: if we are to address the transformation of Europe, we have to start with the question of who will bear responsibility for it and what impact it will have on whom. Because we won't be able to handle the greatest challenges without a two-way movement that combines politics with democratic grassroots action. The key word for the present and for the immediate future should thus be 'balance', as 'equality' has lost much of its value after years of misuse. It is simply not feasible to let those who are responsible for the lion's share of the planet's destruction profit from its destruction while everyone else is advised to tighten their belts and carry out individual improvements. A similar reasoning should apply to most areas that in some way impinge on our everyday life, such as housing, education, healthcare, and public space in general.

It is the unjustly stratified access to public debate that helps to stir up and reawaken the demons that many people have thought were long dead. What European society so desperately needs nowadays is a chance to take a deep breath and start thinking beyond the present day, a chance to see itself differently, in a different constellation and social order. A hundred years after the introduction of the eight-hour working day we are unable to state clearly that we would like to work for half that time at most and perhaps might prefer to spend the rest of the time with our nearest and dearest. Dozens of years after the point when housing became the number one European issue, everyone who spends more than 40 per cent of their income on their accommodation is at risk of homelessness. And had we predicted in the first third of the twentieth century that in the twenty-first education would be only for the few, the then democrats would have thought us idiots or fools. But it is happening anyway. And it was only a few years ago that climate change was also widely regarded as a hysterical lie.

Today, as I gaze at the faces of my children, I see mainly happiness. Happiness about the fact that I can live a relatively contented life. But this makes me all the more aware that I share this privilege with a small select group. Yet Europe used to be a place that served as the model of progress. All too often, though, our European desire for a better life was predicated on the suffering of others. The planet that is 'on fire' thus offers an opportunity to learn from our mistakes, to learn to view the world from perspectives that are not so obvious and make use of them. The future depends on the degree to which we are able to communicate crucial issues with particular regard for the needs of those whom these crises affect rather than of those who benefit from them, be it in economic or political terms. Only then can we hope for a future that won't be just for the richest. Only then can we start building a Europe that will minimise differences rather than amplify them. And only then can we believe in a Europe that will, once again, be a place of safety and solidarity for every single member of society.

Translated from the Czech by Julia Sherwood

My Dream for Europe

Janne Teller

My Dream for Europe is a house. A big house with many rooms, some rooms larger than others, some even huge, while some are smaller, and a few very tiny indeed. The house spans several floors, has numerous staircases and a multitude of long and winding corridors.

It's a magic house, both majestic and mysterious: wherever you look it shifts. It's made out of a panoply, yes seemingly endless number of different materials, ranging from Swedish oaks over Hungarian marble to Portuguese tiles. At every turn of a hallway, there is novelty, with some parts running hushed and supple like valley meadows, some echoing the sharpness of granite, and others akin to walking in forests or up sweetly rolling hills, while yet a few flooded aisles must be jetéd across as fast-flowing river streams. The colours along the corridors go from the more greyish white and brown of the north over infinite green shades from light spring-frog to dark beer-bottle, to red, pink, lilac and turquoise along the waterline, all onto the more auburn and burned sand at the southernmost tips. Some staircases spiral, others are rectangular, some appear endlessly horizontal with just a few finger-widths for steps, while others rise almost vertically towards the sky.

Each room is unlike any other, wondrously, fascinatingly

unalike. The language differs, the music, the food, the style, the habits, the nature, the topography. Even within each room, there are still further, yes myriads of particularities. Every time you walk a step or skew your head, your eyes will catch something they won't see elsewhere. Or may see, but in another form, sometimes with disparities so small you can hardly depict them, only your senses will tell you they are there.

What is amazing with this house is that it's at one with all its divergencies. It defines itself a *House of Variation*. Also, the people vary: some are taller than others, some heavier, some are darker, some lighter, some wear glasses, others not. Some prefer lots of rules and would never cross a path without obtaining an official permit authorising their passing. Others prefer the wilderness of freedom: to walk, sleep and live wherever and in whichever way they desire. Some people believe in one god, some in another, and yet others believe in the same god but have different forms of expressing their beliefs. And there are also many people who believe in no god at all. They all get along, and why shouldn't they?

A love of subtle quality is what all inhabitants of the house have in common. There is no showing off, there is a passion everywhere for the true value of the less ostentatious. Of the people, of the arts, of politics, of anything and everything! The particular pride of the house is that it can hold so many contrarieties and yet be one of harmony – because all the differences are equally respected. All the many variations of subtle quality.

Most respected is life. All life. The aim of the house is not to get bigger or richer. But to ensure the *livability* of all within, as well as beyond the house. So much so that all progress is measured in the livability of humans, of animals, of trees, plants and flowers, of the environment which, it is finally recognised, human livability depends upon: so much so that no product is allowed, no activity, unless its use of, or negative consequences for, the natural habitat is offset in equal measure.

Laid to rest forever are plastics and all other chemicals that aren't easily degradable, or whose long-term biological effects are unknown. In the *House of Livability*, the market forces work to protect the environment because, finally, the true price for the wellbeing of planet Earth has been set and incorporated into all human interventions.

No longer is development measured in economic growth, figures or statistics, virtual or other abstruse scopes. Livability is everything's resonance. Does a motion add to the livability of one, of all? Of the house, of its surroundings, of other houses? Of all living beings, of the planet, the universe?

It is understood that no true wealth exists where poverty sprawls. No happiness is possible where misery abounds. No joy where one person wins and the many lose. Where one person is considered to be worth more than another. Where different rules apply to different people, whether man or woman, old or young, white or of colour, single-sexed or many-sexed or of whichever variety they may choose to be. Of one or another religion, or of none. One or another culture. It is understood that the freedom of one person is sacred, so that the freedom of one person extends itself as far as, yet never beyond, the mark where it infringes upon the freedom of another.

It is a house of ample spaciousness because it was at some point understood that after a certain level, human livability stands in opposite proportion to the number of people, and once upon a time the number of people had made the house so crammed that livability reduced. There had been no more room for the wilderness of nature, and that very wilderness is the essence of the livability of both the house itself and all other houses as well as of the very ground on which all houses stand. By encouraging fewer human offspring, the house has only *one tenth* of its earlier population, as has all other houses around the world. Instead, the number of trees, of flowers, of birds, animals and insects have grown into a truly wild outback that is revered and protected and worshipped as truly sacred to the house.

Abstraction has been understood to be beneficial when it comes to the imagination, philosophy and astronomy, but very unhealthy when indulged in by the worlds of finance or technology. The house was in no doubt that derivative upon derivative of detachment in the realm of financial affairs had led to a gambling syndrome, which no material work could ever compete with. It was banned, of course! Real livability through *real-world* income has since soared to equal out excess inequalities. Pecuniary affairs have been regulated to turn unhealthy to healthy by rooting them deeply in real-world grounds. Thus, they have also become comprehensible for all: investments are once again actual, discernable engagements.

Technology too was seen to have gone astray in life-unhinging levels of obscurity. A screen between you and life is reduced living. And since there was no meaningful answer to the question of what meaningful lives humans would live if artificial intelligence able to carry out all human functions came into being, that road was abandoned in favour of the substantial: In the house, livability is thought to depend to a great degree on that which can be perceived by the senses, on that which can be felt, smelled, tasted, heard or seen. Life through a screen has been given up in favour of embodied life.

It is a house that has found a balance in coexistence, so that all people within all rooms are happy to be a part of the abode. Even the annexe of the house at the Western front, which once voted to depart and make a deep impassable moat between itself and the house, changed its mind and resolved to return. A resolution that not only the inhabitants of the annexe, but also the inhabitants of the rest of the house were very happy about. And things turned out like that simply because the chieftains in the house finally realised that each room had some of their own specific challenges and conditions, and therefore each room should be allowed to make a few specific rules regarding the colour of their interior, the placement of their furniture or, as in the case of the much-valued annexe: regarding the crossing of their doorsteps.

The house takes pride not just in its truly impressive achievements in art, science, philosophical thinking, governance and democratic institutions, but even more so in making up for any wrongs in near or distant pasts that it may have imposed on any person or place within or outside of its own walls. It is a house that takes pride in having changed all its trade, agricultural and other policies, all its political support systems and alliances, so as to ensure that all other houses will attain such livability, such safety, that the inhabitants of all those other houses have no more need to seek sanctuary elsewhere.

But it goes without saying, that should one or another being have a need for shelter, the house will naturally open its door, because what else is life for? Because the very meaning of life is understood to lie in improving the livability and livelihood of each and every one.

My dream for Europe is this house: *The House of Variations, The House of Subtle Quality, The House of Livability. The European House.*

Europe Day or Bloody Thursday

Maarja Kangro

'IGNORANCE,' SHE SAID, 'this was what they intended to block.'

'Can you actually do that?' Myshina, the journalist, asked. 'Block ignorance, by political means?'

Tüüne Kivi smiled.

'You mean whether it's legitimate? Compatible with democracy? Compatible with a citizen's right to give their vote to an ignorant person? Well, after all the things we'd been through – the climate crisis; the deforestation crisis; the constitutional crises all around Europe; the near-abolishment of human rights; bankruptcies and a breakdown in international cooperation – it wasn't the moment to philosophise about whether ignorance really is as ignorant as we think. You do know the extent of what was happening in Europe thirty years ago, don't you?'

'I do,' Myshina said. 'I mean, I've read about it. The Brown Years. The period of far-right movements, populism, inexpertise.'

'Right. The revolt against experts, as one famous European physicist put it back then. The Brits even had a minister who said the people of Britain had had enough of experts.'

Myshina shook her head in disbelief. She was a bit distracted by the glittering azure powder on Tüüne's cheeks. A greyish blue – bizarre, but beguiling. The EU's spring vogue 2050.

Tüüne noticed her glance, smirked, and turned to the audience.

'I'm sure you've heard that Europe was about to crumble. Brexit. The constitutional changes. God. You've read about Brexit?'

Some audience members nodded.

'Initially, we were talking about a wave of right-wing populism and far-right movements,' Tüüne said, 'and then, before we knew it, the word "wave" had become a euphemism.'

'Because it was a storm?' Myshina said.

'Well, what started out as a wave eventually became a kind of plateau. A new norm of ignorance, intolerance, and exclusion. Sure, it had started before that. Le Pen, Orbán, Lega Nord, Prawo i Sprawiedliwość, EKRE in my country, the evil clowns. To them, the bureaucrats in Brussels and Luxembourg were the embodiment of evil.'

'But the liberal elites *had* made mistakes.' Myshina said.

'Oh yes. Those were the old clichés rolled out. The liberal global elites that had neglected the concerns of the suffering classes. The educated or wealthy mobile ones versus the poor immobile ones who were meant to remain in their homeland. Again, the lucky rootless were the ones to blame! A new parodic version of "Blut und Boden",[1] wasn't it?

'Sure, the elites were more mobile than the poorly educated classes. But more than anything, it was an issue of mental mobility over mental immobility. There were loads of migrant workers who turned to nationalism. The construction workers from my country migrated a lot and still voted for the far-right. But they weren't alone, far from it! Many people from the uneducated classes were travelling just for fun. Far from being forced to migrate for work, they were sunbathing in India and Egypt. It was the immobile *mind* that caused problems.

'Now, for many, nationalism was the only answer. There were liberals who proposed liberal nationalism – a soothing sort of nationalism to placate the unlucky immobile classes with their identity crises. One's nation, or ethnicity, proved the perfect rock to cling to in the fear of collective disintegration, rootlessness, lack of recognition.

'Nationalism was the last resort for the deprived ones. Or for those who felt themselves deprived of something: of meaning, education, of the safety of stable values?'

'And this was bullshit. The situation was getting worse. The – well, how can I put it – the immobile, bigoted ones were getting more than their fair share. And for a while, everybody was vying for their votes, so you could hear this general whining: the liberal elites just don't get it, they still fail to address the *people*. The mythical "people", the voters of the far-right who even didn't make up a fifth of the electorate in my country! Give them this and give them that, and they will finally understand. In the beginning, they may restrict the rights of LGBT people, deny climate change, build fences on the borders and force women to give birth, but after a while, they will learn! No, this was bullshit. The far-right ministers, at least in my country, were so uneducated, so unprofessional! It was almost impossible to find a candidate from our far-right party who hadn't been suspected of tax fiddling or even greater criminal offences. Those politicians weren't ever going to change. And yet, they would change something, and that was the constitution.

'This was the storm that swept over Europe: a constitutional threat. The separation of powers was in some countries literally demolished.

'They had referendums planned on Poxit and Huxit. Yeah, Est-exit was considered in my country. It looked like the end of international climate policies; doomsday had arrived, or so it seemed. And then, the riots and strikes started. The revolt of the elites, as some people called them.

'By the slimmest of margins, in some countries, the enlightened parties won. In others, the incompetent coalitions kept breaking up. And then the opposition came up with this slogan. My country was the first to see it, to be honest. "More enlightenment, less democracy", that was what they said. And all of a sudden, this attitude started to spread all over Europe. Actually, something like that had happened before, decades earlier, when Europe refused to let Tsipras have his referendum about the bailout conditions for Greece... but nobody remembers that.'

'And then they changed the electoral system!' Myshina shrieked, exhilarated now.

'Right. Nobody was deprived of the right to vote. Quite the opposite. Certain people got *more* votes than before.'

'Isn't it altogether an appalling concept?' Myshina said. 'This fluid aristocracy?'

Tüüne smiled. Her blue skin sparkled in the sunlight.

'Meritodemocracy is what we call it. It involved a lot of testing at the voting age. An IQ test, several empathy tests, the "scope of empathy" questionnaire. They checked young people's reasoning abilities, language skills, knowledge of history. They tested their capacity for compassion and their ability to cooperate. And, of course, a person's understanding and willingness to accept complex solutions. Those who scored highly enough got one more vote. Those who scored the highest, roughly the top ten per cent, got three votes. And then there was more testing at the age of 30. The same stuff, plus an evaluation of your education up to that point. Education might not exclusively indicate high IQ-scores, but it demonstrates consistency. Again, if you scored highly enough, you'd get one more vote.'

'Isn't that scary? You've reimplemented a class-society!'

Tüüne shrugged nonchalantly.

'That was the way to prevent Nazis or other extremists from taking power again, and indeed it hasn't happened since. Not yet. Europe hasn't fallen apart, it still has its currency, and there's even more freedom for migration within the Union. Well, some people call it a federation now, as Europe is much more federal than it used to be. Of course, it seemed scary at first, this voting system, I agree. But many find it motivating, intellectually stimulating. And then, empathy isn't limited to the upper classes. Anyone's child can be empathic, can't they?'

'But your people don't even vote secretly anymore?' Myshina said. 'They can't even hide in a polling booth?'

Tüüne gave an amused smile.

'Of course they can. The default option is still the secret vote, either electronically or physically, but they've added an option of 'transparent vote': anyone who wants can vote in the Glass Booth. They can click on the name of their candidate so that this name will appear on the huge screen above the booth. Oh, you see, there's Paolo in the cabin, and he voted for Marianne! Or, if they prefer the digital elections, they can opt for the online "transparent vote". Nobody is forced to do that, but for a while and especially among some young progressive people, it became kind of hip, I must admit.'

'Would any of you do that?' Myshina said, turning to the audience.

Some young people mumbled something that sounded like a tentative affirmation. A middle-aged guy with a grey ponytail said, 'Stop! Put a stop to all this right now!'

'I see,' said Myshina.

'I've done it a few times. Voted publicly, I mean,' Tüüne said, 'and it feels good. But another thing I wanted to say, to clear up any misconceptions. We still have ethnicities and nationalities. We still have different cultural preferences. People are not deprived of their ethnic identity. In fact, the opposite is true! They can have several at once. We've got the ethnicity and nationality apps. Very good tutors if you want to delve deeply into a national culture. Anything that might appear violent or discriminatory in a cultural tradition is, of course, removed. Or people have to give their consent that in a restricted space and time, they agree to succumb to such cultural conditions. And, surprise-surprise, most people, I would even say, an overwhelming majority, prefer to stick more or less to the nationality and ethnicity attributed to them at birth. It doesn't look like ethnic or national cultures will evaporate: I think many people naturally prefer to have "slow identities". But all this about cultural and national roots is more a logistical problem than a political one. And having identified the genes responsible for the skin pigmentation…'

'Exactly!' Myshina exclaimed. 'I wanted to ask you about the designer babies! It sounds so non-European!'

'Ah. It's legal, but it's prohibitively expensive to the vast majority of people. It's undertaken only in cases to prevent certain hereditary conditions, or by the hyper-rich. However, this option has done a lot to dissolve the prevailing concept of race. And we have to acknowledge that this is thanks to them. I mean, thanks to this pioneering group of people, enlightened tycoons who first decided to bear children with different skin colour to their own. Honey-coloured, chocolate-coloured babies were born to pale-skinned parents. After that, then, some rich African parents also decided to have white babies, who were so cute-looking!'

Myshina gave her a horrified look. 'What do you mean? Forgive me, but this sounds like a…'

'A what?' Tüüne seemed amused. 'A fad? A step too far? Skin colour as an aesthetic choice can obviously also cause tension and discrimination, but at least we have proved how arbitrary, how fluid any "colour identity" is. And then, most of those who could afford the skin colour manipulation, still don't opt for it. Again, it's easier when someone else, like nature, decides these things for you, isn't it? And your offspring can't reproach you personally later, ha!'

Myshina laughed politely, and some young people in the audience laughed, too.

'So, on that highly polemical point,' the journalist said to the room, 'and before touching briefly upon Ms Kivi's own professional field, financing the fine arts in the EU, do we have any questions from the audience? About this peculiar electoral system, maybe?'

'It's always the perverts with the money,' called an old lady from the back.

Tüüne nodded slightly, giving the audience an encouraging smile.

A young girl stood up in the second row, waving for the microphone. As an assistant approached her, the man with a thin ponytail from before stood up in the first row, took a step towards the stage and then leapt up onto it. Most of the audience seemed to think it was part of the act.

Tüüne Kivi was later quite sure that she hadn't jumped back to hide behind Myshina; that is, her course-mate Marina who had adopted that silly Dostoyevskian name for the show. Tüüne had always been the more talented one, nobody could deny that, and the sketch for the Europe Day 2019, Freedom Square, Tallinn, had also been mostly her idea. Marina had wanted to do some comical sketch about the European elections, but now really wasn't the right time, what with EKRE in power.

No, Tüüne didn't hide, and she certainly didn't push Marina in front of her. But she was indeed trying to get away from the maniac, since it was obvious that he was coming for her and not for Marina. After all, she was the 'EU alien'. It's possible that people invent their own memories, and that this is why she remembered the strange moment of sensing Marina's navy linen jacket in front of her. Marina's back in front of her, though it didn't happen like that.

It was all so absurd: the pseudo-medieval knife and the sweaty idiot, vile like an insect in his white T-shirt. It was surreal and real, and it all happened so fast.

Suddenly there was bright blood all over the stage and everybody was screaming. Was Tüüne screaming, too? The guy had slashed Marina's cheek, but Tüüne couldn't see that yet. There was so much blood she thought she might be wounded as well, but she wasn't. There was the blue May sky and there were the lime trees beside the yellow church. That's also where the police cars were.

The guy was shot down by a young policeman who was later reproached for losing his nerve and risking people's lives. The ponytailed man hadn't announced his attack in advance on social media. He did have a Facebook account and had indeed joined some far-right-leaning groups on there, declaring also that he had voted for EKRE at the elections on 3 March 2019, but he was far from politically active. He had lost his job at a car rental company half a year earlier and his parents said he had been battling with depression since primary school. He had a three-year-old daughter, but she lived with her mother.

The press secretary for EKRE said the party couldn't be held responsible for the acts of its supporters. He also claimed that the Europe Day sketch of the theatre students had been an outright provocation.

Marina said she would quit theatre school if they didn't find a cure for her facial palsy. She never hinted to anything cowardly in Tüüne's behaviour, and Tüüne had a text based on their sketch published in a literary magazine. She put Marina's name there as well, although she thought she should have been the sole author. However, for months after the attack, Tüüne continued to see the navy-blue linen fabric in front of her. She was crouching behind it.

Where did this memory come from? Would it keep

coming back forever? There were times when she thought she would talk it over with Marina. Yes, she would ask her directly, when they next met. And they did meet, and they talked about Marina's new bike, and, of course, envisaged the collapse of the government again, and Tüüne didn't mention the Europe Day episode. She felt happy and strong as they parted, for a few blocks. And then it crept back again.

Notes

1. Blood and soil (German: Blut und Boden) is a nationalist slogan popularised by the prominent Nazi theorist Richard Walther Darré in 1930.

Things That Have Nothing to Do with Reason

Saara Turunen

I was in Barcelona. I spent Christmas there with my partner, then took a flight back home to Helsinki. On the plane, I noticed a blonde woman with a foreign-looking partner. I looked at her surreptitiously and wondered if her life was like mine. The woman had mid-length hair and an expensive-looking handbag. Next to her sat two beautiful children. They were watching cartoons and the woman was drinking champagne, sure of her worth. It looked as if her life was under control. I wondered if the woman ever felt that everything was about to collapse. That's a feeling I have often, and so I'm almost always restless.

I met my partner ten years ago – it was morning, and we were coming out of a club as the sun was rising. I was studying at drama school in Barcelona and spending all my time partying. The man persuaded me to go with him to an after-party. I feigned indifference, though I had fallen in love with him on the spot and would have followed him down a well if he'd asked. It was his smile. It was exciting, the way he smiled almost all the time. I wasn't used to that. I – and all the people I had met up to that point in my life – only smiled in special circumstances. I also found the man handsome, and while perhaps it sounds smarter to say that looks don't matter, that inner beauty is the thing, real beauty has an enchanting effect, like a lamp that makes flying insects go crazy; so I let myself be drawn into my partner's aura and for some reason he let me stay.

Now we live in the Sant Gervasi district, on a street called Marià Cubí. Or rather, my partner lives there and I visit him from Finland whenever I can. Sometimes I have to be in my home country for a long time, working and dedicating myself to art, but then, when there's a gap in my schedule, I book a flight immediately and travel to see him. I'm not proud of this constant flying around. I know it's stupid and destroys the planet. But I have to see him; otherwise I sink into despair, buried alive, and that's not nice at all.

My home country is tucked up at the back of Europe, in a corner, and if I tried to travel using another method, I'd have to take a boat and then a coach and a bus and another bus and so on, until finally, I'd arrive so many days later that it would be time to set off home again. Once I made the journey by coach with a friend. First, we went through the Baltics, then continued via Croatia to Italy, and from there to Spain. It took about two weeks in all and was really tiring. The coaches were full of Polish men who drank a brown drink that looked like home-brew out of 1.5-litre bottles, and then passed out on the floor. At the Hungarian border, the police came to take them away in an armoured car, and they looked as floppy as spaghetti as they were marched to the vehicle.

One option would have been to leave all this behind, but I have tried that, and it didn't work. I told my partner that we should separate, on the grounds of rationality. I had weighed things up, put them in order of priority, and said to myself, come on, please, focus on your career, you can't go squandering your life chasing after some foreigner. You have studied in the best art schools, dreamt big, and frittered away student loans in the bar across the street, so don't let it all go to waste. Besides, the man smokes – tobacco as well as grass – his shoes are falling apart, and he doesn't often remember to shave. He plays PlayStation and eats red meat at every meal; he doesn't know how to place the knife and fork next to the plate in the proper way, on top of the napkin, instead dumping his cutlery on the table randomly, no matter how many times I've told him it's not nice.

But my partner does not care about middle-class habits. I didn't either when I was young. The bourgeois desire for the proper placement of knives and forks snuck up on me after I turned thirty. It sat at the head of the dining table, scanned the room and said: *New curtains and cushion covers are in order here. Wine and sparkling wine require their own glasses, and napkins should be made of the finest calico, if you please.* I tried not to listen, but it didn't work. Such bourgeois ways were a memory of childhood, a strange shadow that took up residence in my flat and demanded all sorts of things. Probably it was to do with the fact that death was drawing closer, and its inevitability began to be frightening. I hoped to be able to create a sense of security by getting curtains I could lean on if everything else fell apart and collapsed. And so, I left my partner, and the new curtains became useful. I cried on the floor for days, clinging to the high-quality fabric, thinking only of my partner whom I had left in the street by a cafe, looking broken. My mind was black and, from somewhere deep in my soul, a thought arose: I have made the worst mistake of my life. Love songs began to sound strangely rational. Lyrics that went: *I'll die if I can't be with you, I'll jump off Ponte Vecchio and be carried away by the water,* like in the opera *Tosca.* I'd never been into love songs. I thought people who spent their time on such rubbish weren't right in the head, and now, out of nowhere, I was one of them.

I also understood, bitterly, that the career I had believed in and for which I had trained did not exist. Making art demands only that you do it; the setting doesn't really matter. I did sense something along those lines when I rented a small, expensive studio for myself in a basement in the city centre. In it, I put a functional desk and an old pewter mug I had found in my great-aunt's attic and which I believed my grandfather had used to drink from in the war. Now the pewter mug was my pencil pot; pencils waited for their user next to a pile of paper, but no one took up either pencil or paper because, suddenly, I had nothing to say. I was missing my partner. I sat in the emptiness of the basement, stared with glazed eyes out of the small window in the grip of a crippling sorrow because I couldn't escape the thought that I had made the worst mistake of my life. My partner loved me. He had said it quite clearly, though he had no reason to do so; there was nothing lovable about me. Never in my little life had I got anyone else to say anything like that. Mostly, men gave me a wide berth. I had understood that, in their view, there was something frightening about me. I shouted my opinions and planned art projects instead of listening to their musings and supporting them in their endeavours. I had seen these men become horrified and flee the scene. They stopped answering text messages. They took up with some nice woman who listened. For some strange reason, only in my partner's mind was there nothing scary about me being loud-mouthed and having ideas. On the contrary, my partner liked calling me 'boss', and laughed about it.

After a few weeks, I stopped going to the basement. It was damn cold down there, and I didn't dare use the toilet because it was behind a storage area full of cages and brought the film *Trainspotting* to mind. I left my functional desk and pewter mug in the care of another artist and heard later that the building had suffered water damage. Brown water had flooded the basement and the pewter mug sailed away. So leaving that hidey-hole was the right decision, and one that never caused me the regret I felt upon leaving my partner, that decent man who couldn't lay the table properly. How important were table manners, at the end of the day? That's what I wondered, as my despair became so deep and the high-quality curtains so frayed that I decided to coax my partner back. I travelled to his city. I called his phone. I went to his home and slept in his bed, even as my conscience troubled me, perhaps because I understood that my solution was bad, in a way; that there was something really senseless about it. But I couldn't do anything about all that, for these matters have nothing to do with reason.

I have been asked to write a text about the future of Europe. This is because I have been invited to a festival due to take place in Croatia next summer and I understand interesting artists from all the European Union countries have been invited. A summer festival sounds fun and I'm flattered to have been asked, so I replied positively to the letter, and then started to write this. I'm not sure what this has to do with Europe or the world, but something, I guess, since I do live in Europe, as well as in the world, and I know that a lot of things are going in the wrong direction. The icebergs are melting and polar bears sinking into the sea. Forests are being felled so we can have more paper, so my home country can sell big rolls of it abroad and show off about the ever-decreasing levels of unemployment in our country, even though the unemployed have just been tidied away from the statistics, made to take part in job-creation schemes that involve carving wooden butter knives and making mosaic trivets. But in spite of all that, I still feel like writing about my partner, and how I fly to meet him on a cheap airline flight, even though I know this only fosters more destruction. On top of this, the idea is to fly me and all the other artists to this summer festival, the one I'm writing this for. So in that respect, the text also rests on shaky foundations, adding to the lurking sensation of collapse.

When I met my partner, he didn't know how to use a vacuum cleaner. He only had a broom and a mop at home, and a cleaner who used them while my partner smoked on the lower bunk of his bunk bed. When he moved to his own place, he was left holding a broom, baffled, not knowing what to do with it. I headed for the shopping centre and bought a vacuum cleaner. In my partner's view, it was a useless, noisy object, but he still carried the box home. When I went to install the dust-bag, I noticed it was already full. I couldn't understand how a vacuum cleaner in a sealed box could have been used, but perhaps it had been used as a display model or someone had bought it, vacuumed at home, then returned it. I said, we've got to return the vacuum cleaner, and my partner said he had known nothing good would come of it. We took it back to the shopping centre; my partner stopped to browse the perfumes while I went to return the vacuum cleaner, but they wouldn't believe me. I've noticed I can't really talk to Spanish people. Perhaps there's something too direct in the way I approach them and they're startled. I was about to start shouting when my partner arrived to help. He flashed his best smile at the salesperson and the vacuum cleaner was exchanged immediately. We went home with the new one and my partner said I needed to learn to talk a bit more nicely if I wanted people to listen to me. 'Jesus,' I said. The vacuum cleaner stayed and, in the end, my partner even learned to like it. Occasionally he'll dig it out and hoover up our breakfast crumbs.

Whenever I'm in Barcelona, we always eat lunch together. My partner leaves work at three o'clock and once he's rushed back to Marià Cubí Street on his scooter, it's already easily four. In my home country, we eat lunch much earlier, and in Barcelona, the clock is an hour behind Finland. And so by four o'clock, I'll usually have been pacing around the flat for the last two hours unable to write because I'm so hungry. I do like having to make real meals to eat, and I like to always lay the table nicely, setting out the knives and forks with care, and how we eat opposite each other and talk about our days. I think that if I were to live like this all the time, I'd throw the pots and pans out of the window and flee, but because I only live like this occasionally, it seems like a game, a bit like when, as children, we would go outside and make soup out of grass and muddy water and eat it sitting at the edge of the sandpit.

Translated from the Finnish by Emily Jeremiah

Our Mediterranean Mother

Leïla Slimani

WHAT IF THE FUTURE of freedom were being written in the Maghreb? What if we looked to the other side of the Mediterranean to find the most exciting collective adventures, to discern the outline of a new form of democracy where people questioned violence, economic power and the development of society in a new way?

Between 2011 and 2019, popular uprisings changed the destinies of Tunisia and then Algeria. I was on Avenue Bourguiba when the Jasmine Revolution began, and I have some extraordinary memories of those moments shared with the Tunisian people. I covered Ben Ali's Tunisia as a journalist from 2008 to 2011, and I had the feeling at the time that this country and its youth were dying. Young people were being driven to illegal emigration and suicide by the nation's ills: police brutality, the economic crisis, endemic corruption and mass unemployment. Tunisia had been undermined so deeply and systematically by its ruling regime that it was hard to see a way out of the situation. In Algeria, similar causes produced comparable effects. And, there too, there was a sense of amazement, among observers and the protesters themselves. As the Algerian journalist and author Kamel Daoud put it: 'We had forgotten that we were a people, and in the street, we were united once again, amid joy and laughter.'

In Europe, nobody had forecast the rise of these popular movements because it is nearly ten years since the European Union stopped taking an interest in the Maghreb. When I was a student, the Mediterranean was still talked about as a sphere of influence on Europe. Remember Turkey presenting its arguments for joining the club of 27 member states? Even Morocco did not exclude the possibility of gradually joining the Union. There's a story that King Hassan II hired teams of Moroccan and Spanish engineers to make a presentation – at a meeting with Jacques Delors, who was president of the European Commission at the time – for his plan to build a bridge that would connect Africa to the Old Continent. In 2008, the French president Nicolas Sarkozy wanted to pursue this dream of bringing together the peoples of the North and South by launching the Union for the Mediterranean. But no solid union could ever be forged with a band of dictators like Muammar Gaddafi, Bashar al-Assad and Hosni Mubarak.

I am from the Maghreb; I am from the Mediterranean. My attachment to Europe was built across that sea. For me, *mare nostrum* was not a border and not yet a cemetery; it was the outline of a community. In Homer, the Mediterranean is *hygra keleutha*, the liquid road, a space of transition and sharing. It is our common heritage. Ulysses made stopovers on the coast of Africa just as he did in the Greek islands. When I first visited Spain, Portugal and Italy, I was struck by this feeling of familiarity. So how can we explain Europe's current inability to face that sea? How can we understand the way it has deliberately turned its back on the Mediterranean, when this southward tropism is one of the most fortunate aspects of our continent? We have lost the Mediterranean and betrayed that essential part of our identity. How humiliating and how tragic, those boats that roam the sea, unwanted. How devastating to see the youth of the Maghreb and Africa turning away from the continent that has rejected them and let them down.

The Austrian author Stefan Zweig devoted a large part of his critical work to the European question. In an article published before the Second World War, he writes that a Russian exile once told him: 'In the old days, a man had only a body and a soul. Now, he needs a passport too, otherwise he is not treated like a man.' And Zweig, who saw the European continent sink into the horrors of fascism and genocide, adds: 'The first visible manifestation of our century's moral epidemic was xenophobia: the hatred or, at the very least, the fear of the other. Everywhere, people defended themselves against the foreigner, they excluded and separated him. All those humiliations that before had been reserved for criminals were now inflicted on travellers.' And still today, the question of migration is fundamental, central, because the future of our continent will be decided in terms of our capacity to welcome and also to think about the Other.

The European Union, built on the ruins of the Second World War, was intended to be an incarnation of pacifism and the virtues of dialogue. Whether through Schengen or Erasmus, it championed the ground-breaking idea of a future based on reducing borders and encouraging the circulation of people, products and ideas. It is easy to forget this now, but when the European project was first conceived by its founding fathers, it was profoundly innovative, even subversive. Turning its back on a warlike, dog-eat-dog vision of the world, the European Union was designed to promote mutual assistance and cooperation. It seems such a sad waste that this democratic ideal is now considered by some to be a sort of outdated, rancid utopianism, while nationalist speeches are cheered, and walls are being built on our doorsteps.

But the EU also bears some responsibility for what has happened to it. During the last ten years, the Union has too often renounced its own moral principles, providing fuel for nationalist and populist arguments. Europe's leaders have demonstrated shameful cynicism by constantly prioritising finance and economics over the construction of a genuine 'European people'. The management of the 2008 economic crisis in Greece constituted the EU's first moral failure: by showing its reactionary side, it reduced Europe to a union that was essentially commercial, cold and heartless, embodied by a dominant elite obsessed with profit. Man's indifference to man seemed to become the norm. The second stage in the EU's fall came in 2015, with the migrant crisis. The image of those masses of people fleeing poverty and war and coming up against Europe's haughty indifference left a deep wound in the hearts of many of us. Even today, this continent that sees itself as a lighthouse for the world is, in reality, incapable of fighting against the slavery at its doorstep, the death on its shores, the poverty within its borders.

Faced with populists promising simple answers and playing on people's fears, the EU must cast aside its fear of what it is and boldly proclaim that utopia is possible. It must reduce inequality, improve the democratic process, fight climate change, and welcome refugees fleeing wars and poverty. To be European is to believe that we are, at once, diverse and united, that the Other is different but equal. That cultures are not irreconcilable; that we are capable of building a dialogue and a friendship by seeking out what we have in common. The universalism of the Enlightenment must be at the heart of the European project.

It was probably in Europe that the awareness of what is today called 'globalisation' was first forged. Stefan Zweig wrote that, after the First World War, the intellectuals of the

Old Continent were both enthusiastic and anxious about the fact that the destiny of the different peoples was now so closely linked: 'Humanity, as it spread across the earth, became more intimately interconnected, and today it is shaken by a fever, the entire cosmos shivering with dread.' European integration was driven by that awareness: the great problems of tomorrow will not be resolved at a national scale. Only by combining our efforts will we find solutions to the challenges of the future, and the best example of this is obviously the planet's ecological ultimatum.

It seems to me that Europe must look southward, with interest, respect and passion. It must look to those shores, too, in order to move on to the next chapter in its history; to cease defining itself as an old colonising power, and to find strength in its egalitarian values. To stop wallowing in nostalgia, and instead pour its energy into inventing a better future. Europe must no longer be defined by Christianity or by exclusive, irreconcilable national identities, but must return to the Greek matrix that unites the two sides of *mare nostrum*. In Greek, the term *Crisis* comes from *crineo*, which means to choose. That's where Europe is now: at a crossroads. And our common future will depend on which path we take next, which moral and philosophical choice we make.

Translated from the French by Sam Taylor

The Quest for Europe's Global Strategic Role

Yvonne Hofstetter

THE OXFORD ENGLISH DICTIONARY defines the word 'atlas' as 'a collection of maps bound between two book covers.' In these times of digitalised knowledge, geography on paper has become a precious treasure on our bookshelves. The world maps we find online can show us the pixelated outline of Europe, a mosaic of colourful mid-sized and small states – with a variety of historical experiences and cultures – adjoined to its eastern neighbours, Russia and China. Both nations have continental reach and, geographically-speaking, Europe is the western portion of the Eurasian landmass. Nevertheless, it has always been seen as being separate from the East. Europe's participation in the North Atlantic Treaty Organisation – NATO – speaks to this, as well as its conceptualisation of human rights, rule of law, democracy, and the social market economy as a unified entity. A set of principles that Russia wants to follow as little as China, and there are signs that America, too, is withdrawing.

A united Europe: nothing but narrative?

Wherever the call for greater European unity flares up, so too does strong opposition. In many ways, online communities and 'social' networks have divided us instead of united us. Designed as product catalogues for the twenty-first century, they have performed a great deception in creating the image of 'social media', because their sole purpose is, in fact, a capitalist one: making money from advertising. The consequences of this are all around us: society is broken down into its separate components, into its smallest atoms. They become a singularity, an isolated individual without a strong sense of group belonging or shared identity. Despite promoting social diversity, the digital era has led to milieu-thinking and the creation of echo chambers, not only on a personal but national level. On top of this, various 'Europes' have emerged: one for Scandinavians, another for those residing on the Mediterranean or those from the Visegrád Group (Czech Republic, Hungary, Poland and Slovakia). Separations like Brexit, or the rise of nationalist movements, are unhappy consequences. It is precisely because we haven't internalised the guiding principles of Europe, in which we would all be able to reach a minimal political consensus, that others now tell us who we are, or what they *think* we are.

Geopolitical sandwich: Europe between two systems

As the wheel of history continues to turn, and earlier certainties fall victim to progress, a new social dynamic emerges. Even the old friendship between Europe and America no longer seems reliable: 'Well, I think we have a lot of foes. I think the European Union is a foe, what they do to us in trade. Now you wouldn't think of the European Union, but they're a foe.'[1] Despite his bad diplomatic style, Donald Trump is not entirely wrong. For decades, Europe has acted as America's 'free rider'. Our ally in the West – and the undisputed global hegemonic power since the fall of the Soviet Union in 1991– has provided Europe with international public goods, the so-called commons, including GPS and the internet. Europe was content to rely on the services provided by the US and even saved billions in investment, money that was later used as a peace dividend to fund social welfare. Therefore, the withdrawal of Donald Trump into Fortress America, held up as a second American decline, is a capital problem, but also a great opportunity for a new world order in which Europe can regain sovereignty on the world stage.

After all, East Asia is becoming a system alternative to the historical West. Unlike Donald Trump, who pursues nothing but 'conservative isolationism [...] and non-interference in the world's conflicts',[2] the Chinese President Xi Jinping has a highly ambitious political goal and tries to control everything and everyone in his quest to realise the 'Chinese dream': everyone should be equally wealthy, only without democracy, without the free press and civil society.

For China to exert more influence over Eurasia, America must be ousted from Europe. In 2012, China launched the 17+1 initiative: a strategic cooperation between China and central and eastern European countries, including the Visegrád Group and the Baltic states. Chinese direct investment in economically relevant resources – such as ports in southern Europe, shares in technology companies, even wineries in France – and the Belt and Road Initiative[3] are the mechanism through which to impose a different political system on Europe. This has created a rift in Europe, and subsequently, joint European human rights declarations against China have become more and more difficult.

In the medium term, digital technologies will allow China to exercise political dominance and military control over newly gained resources. In Europe's West, there is no longer anyone extending a helping hand. And to the East, the threat of great power struggles and high-tech armament is growing. Europe and its guiding principles are under increasing pressure, along with its 'world relations'. This refers to the connectedness not only between the European states, but also the personal connection of Europeans with each other, as well as, of course, the successful coexistence of a European society, expressed in the European motto: *In varietate concordia* – united in diversity.

Doing world politics

Central to this dynamic, Europe needs a vision for the future, a new declaration of its objectives that can guide internal decision-making and enable it to distinguish itself from American or Chinese politics.

'The fact is that the European Union and its predecessor, the European Economic Community (EEC), were not geared towards global political capability. We weren't capable of world politics for a long time. And the circumstances mean that we must strive for global political capacity,' commission president Jean-Claude Juncker said in a speech in 2018. What the goal of such world politics is, comes into focus when we ask ourselves two questions, originally posed by Henry Kissinger: 'What do we really want to achieve? What must we absolutely prevent?'[4] For the purpose of our own reflection, we can go a little further: What role could technology play? An impact-based approach does not begin with the *causa*, but rather always with the desired final state into which Europe will enter.

Europe is still an asset with great potential. If it wanted to, Europe could become a major hegemonic power, not for the whole world, but for its own development, building a strong democratic utopia for the future. Europe's global position could be based on its democratic, liberal and social charisma, with a multilateral policy in close coordination with other democratic states and multi-pronged principles, not only characterised by self-interest, but with a dash of altruism.

Achieving this would not be easy. After all, not all European governments are convinced by the democratic ideal. Doubts must be overcome, and democratic convictions asserted. Complaining, debating, carrying on as before, getting swept up in nostalgia: this is not how democracy is preserved, this is not how it will prevail. Only if a determined democratic policy were to make use of all diplomatic, technological, military and economic resources and tools from across Europe, would there be a chance for it to make an impact.

How do you become a hegemony?

Hegemonic power, we know from history, is based on soft power – the magic that springs from the power of persuasion. We know from history that such power is based on fundamentals. It won't happen of its own accord – and it's expensive because the list of attractions that impart soft power is long. It definitely includes a vibrant economy and market power. Freedom, democracy, rule of law and quality media. A stable currency. Prosperity and a decline in poverty. Internal as well as external security. Peace in Europe. Social permeability and social unity. Diversity and openness. A deep friendship among Europeans and reliable alliances despite independence and autonomy. And new technologies will, of course, be integral.

1. Digital technologies serve Europe's guiding principles

Future European leadership – unlike the Asiatic challenge to the system – will also rely on the European *condition humana* and the image of 'man' as a sovereign individual, which is the basis of every liberal-democratic social order. Its appeal would effectively be safeguarded and defended in the next iteration of digital progress, even against the capitalist claims of American digitalisation evangelists, who, when explaining the matter to a public reduced to the measurable and visible, say that they should have full access to digital surveillance and algorithmic analysis.

Scientists and companies who bring new technologies to market cannot, and should not, be solely in charge of democratic 'compliance'. Politics has only recently begun to hold them to account for the societal effects these new technologies or digital business models can cause. Before 2016 – a year which revealed the abuse potential of digitalisation – it was not within a company's remit to consider the societal or legal compliance of their digital innovations. That has since changed and, in 2018, the European Commission established rules to ensure *responsible* research and innovation, imposing a mandatory ethical, legal and societal impact assessment on every new research project funded by the European Union. But even before scientists attempt to formulate self-imposed obligations in the descriptive language of mathematics and squeeze the European idea into programming code as 'ethics-by-design', ethics consultants and lawyers must have already put to paper what the legal European ethos entails.

European digital technologies are compatible with democracy if they respect the rights and responsibilities of their users. They are compatible if they do not reduce real people to a data set. They are compatible if they go beyond monitoring and controlling people. Instead, we need to reconsider fundamental rights in the digital age, recognising that online profiles, smartphones – even the chip at the end of a fingertip – are as inseparable from people today as a cardiac catheter or artificial hip.

2. New technologies for the security of Europe

The central element of European soft power would be the provision of the 'commons' at a low cost.[5] Peace and security are also an essential part of these commons, in the case of European future policy, the *Pax Europaea*. The European Union must be committed to keeping 700 million Europeans safe. This concern for the public good cannot only be political, it demands defence and military security as well. It is not enough to simply support digital technologies for Europe's greater economic competitiveness. After all, defence and crisis management will be increasingly supported by cognitive machines. If the states to the east of Europe modernise their arsenals, arm military robots and develop increasingly autonomous weapons systems, Europe needs to be able to respond, while also keeping an eye on the geostrategic significance of digital progress. Europe should not give itself over to the naïve hope that doctrines for the defence of the future would be a by-product of civil research and development. This is not the case, which is why digital technologies should be specifically explored for their ability to change the conflicts of the future.

3. Soft power through innovation

Innovation is also a determining factor for hegemony. This does not only include technological innovations; innovation can also be bureaucratic, legal, cultural or economic.[6] This is why European world policy needs to assess new technologies for their political impact. Innovation doesn't only make you more attractive, it also solves problems. And Europe has plenty of those. Someone needs to address climate change. The migration pressure from the south. The demographic shift. Urbanisation and its consequences. Social inequality. The fragmentation of society.

Artificial intelligence, in particular, is regarded worldwide as the general-purpose technology of the twenty-first century. The US still dominates in this field. China, South Korea, Russia, Singapore and Israel are all high up on the list of their most promising competitors. A European country is not among them.[7] Nevertheless, it is far from clear who will position themselves as the future front runner, because there is still such a huge gap between the vision of the capabilities of cognitive machines and reality. Up to now, artificial intelligence has provided only selective improvements to everyday life.

Whoever manages to build cognitive machines for a meaningful usage context, and to think of the legal, ethical and social technological consequences of Europe, could take the lead.

The security of the Pax Europaea

European hegemony is the great dream of a Europe that takes a firm democratic and secure stand. It's the desire for a Europe that tells a coherent narrative about itself, before others do so in its place. It is the vision of strength, fuelled by an unwavering guiding principle of *humanitas* and a common strategy for its realisation and protection.

But reality is currently taking a detour through populism, protectionism, nationalism and a good dose of arrogance. Those who love Europe and its guiding principles should not succumb to sadness, but rather gather their strength. Each and every one of us can breathe life back into Europe, build a better future and live humanely and democratically with others. Based on our shared past and visions of the future, we must trust that a unified Europe is the best of all worlds.

Translated from the German by Jen Calleja

Notes

1. Trump, Donald. 2018. Interview: Jeff Glor Interviews Donald Trump in Scotland (Complete). Factba.se. [Online] 14 July 2018. [Quote from: 20 August 2018.] https://factba.se/transcript/donald-trump-jeff-glor-cbs-news-full-interview-july-14-2018.

2. Menzel, Ulrich. 2015. *Die Ordnung der Welt.* (Berlin: Suhrkamp, 2015), p. 888

3. The Belt and Road Initiative (BRI), also referred to as the New Silk Road, is a Chinese infrastructure project to expand trade and facilitate China's ambitions to become a world leader.

4. Ischinger, Wolfgang. 2017. *Vortrag im Bayerischen Hof, München: Zukunftsfragen deutscher und europäischer Sicherheitspolitik.* 2017.

5. Cf. (Menzel, 2015), p. 958

6. Cf. numerous examples in (Menzel, 2015)

7. Horowitz, Michael C., et al. 2018. *Strategic Competition in an Era of Artificial Intelligence.* Washington, D.C.: CNAS.ORG, 2018, p. 8

I Can Now Tell You My Story

Sofía Kouvelaki

I AM WRITING THIS because, some time ago, I made a promise to a twelve-year-old boy from Afghanistan. His name is Hamid. I promised Hamid I would share his story.

Hamid left by himself from Kandahar in Afghanistan to come to Europe. He left behind his parents, his five brothers, and the terror imposed by the Taliban, who burned his best friend alive before his eyes. It was at that moment Hamid decided to leave his city. Hamid was an excellent student and thought to be the most promising of his siblings. He wanted a chance to have a life, to stop struggling in order to merely survive. He didn't want to live with fear every single day of his life. These were his words to me:

> I have walked all the way to Turkey through the valleys, the mountains and the deserts of three countries. After four months, I reached the coast. I had never seen so much water before. The small boat to Greece was full of people. Women and babies were crying. Thank God, we arrived alive, but we were arrested by the police. I ended up in prison. It is difficult when I think about how many days I was there. What did I do wrong?

Hamid was detained – with another 40 minors – for more than two months in Amygdaleza, a detention centre for refugees in Greece. After being released, he spent five months homeless, living in Pedion tou Areos – one of the largest public parks in the centre of Athens.

> I was alone again. I started sleeping in the park. Every night men would come near me. They would drink beer and do drugs. One night, an old man came and offered me 20 euros to go home with him. I started running to get away. I was scared. I didn't know what to do or where to go. I had no papers, so I was also afraid of the police. I was walking all night long. I tried to ask for help, but no one spoke my language. Someone led me to the centre for homeless people in Omonoia Square. With my very limited English, I understood there was no room, so I had to leave. I started sleeping in one of the corners of the square. On Christmas Day, I met Amadou, who brought me to the HOME Project. That was my best moment in Athens. Everything has changed since then, and I can now tell you my story.

Hamid ended up in one of our shelters, so in a way, he is one of the 'fortunate' lone refugee children. Sadly, this is not the case for the majority of the kids. Hamid is one of the superheroes of Europe's ongoing refugee crisis. He is one of the thousands of children, travelling alone, amidst the biggest demographic shift since the Second World War. They are what we call in official terms 'unaccompanied minors'. The scale of the exodus in which they are moving is momentous. The reasons they travel alone vary. Many have lost their parents during the journey; others are sent away to escape war, poverty or persecution. These children are all in search of a better future. They are undertaking epic journeys that would intimidate even the strongest adult. Travelling alone and unprotected, they are exposed to all sorts of dangers, from child abuse to organ trafficking and sexual exploitation.

Awaiting refugee children on the other side of their journeys are closed borders in Greece, where there is a chronic lack of social welfare facilities and services to accommodate them and provide them with the necessary safety framework.

More than 1,800,000 people have reached Europe since the beginning of 2015.

More than 15,000 lives have been lost while crossing the Mediterranean.

Many of the dead are believed to be children, and many were travelling alone.

The term 'migrant' or 'refugee' crisis cannot begin to depict the complexity of this phenomenon. Forty per cent of refugee arrivals are children. Among those – we don't know exactly how many and this is part of the problem – are thousands of children who travel and arrive in Europe all alone. A large number of these children don't get registered and are left outside of any protection system. 150,000 unaccompanied minors have sought asylum in the European Union since 2015 (Eurostat).

Hamid is one of the 25,081 unaccompanied minors that have been officially registered in Greece since the beginning of 2016. And despite the decrease in refugee arrivals in Greece after the EU Turkey agreement, the number of children travelling and arriving in Greece all alone is increasing. With the borders closed, these children are now trapped in Greece. And the problem is that all the relevant accommodation units have reached full capacity.

As I write, more than 3,700 unaccompanied refugee

children are without a home, and in urgent need of protection and support. They are spread all over the country – living in police stations, detention centres, camps, with no access to basic care, services, and no information on their rights. They are coexisting with adults in appalling living conditions and suffering from all sorts of sexual, physical, emotional and psychological violence.

These children are the victims of a cycle of violence. They start off fleeing from violence, but they often experience violence again when they reach European borders. They often suffer from 'injured hero' syndrome. They managed to arrive in what they thought was the promised land, where they thought their troubles would be over, only to experience more violence, insecurity and abuse. The kids who arrive at our shelters are often more traumatised by the experiences they have had after their arrival in Europe than those they endured during their perilous journey, or at home.

What is a child refugee? He or she is a *child* in urgent need of refuge, a *child* in urgent need of a home. At the HOME Project, we don't work with refugees, we don't work with migrants, we work with children – children who have been marginalised to the point of invisibility. HOME stands for Help, Overcome, Motivate, Empower, which is what we aim to do with every child we work with, every single day. Our mission is to provide support, protection, education and social integration services to children who travel and arrive in Greece all alone. We currently support the operation of eleven shelters (seven of them for boys, two of them for girls and underage mothers with their babies, one for younger boys, and one for over eighteens). A total of 11 shelters for 220 kids, having created more than 140 jobs, half of which are in the refugee community. We have proved, by our actions, that solutions do exist. Solutions are possible.

The HOME Project shelter model is based on three pillars:

1. A holistic network of child protection services covering critical needs such as food, shelter, material and medical provision but also social, legal, mental health support and social integration services. All the children staying in our shelters obtain immediate access to education and attend public school in Greece.

2. We create jobs for refugees as well as Greeks. In order to integrate into any society, people need a home, but they also need a job. Fifty per cent of our shelter staff is comprised of refugees. They become role models for the kids, demonstrating in action that there can be a future for them.

3. We create value for the local economy. There are numerous unused, unrented buildings all over Greece in relatively good condition. We have added value to real estate property while paying minimal rent and alleviating the owners from the infamously high ENFIA Greek property tax.

At the HOME Project, we have created the conditions for a win-win situation both for the child refugees and the Greek population. Our aim is to enable healing environments and platforms of inclusion, skill-building and employment, leading to a more organic bottom-up form of social integration that will facilitate community engagement. As we see it, this is the only way we can fight racism, xenophobia and violent local reactions.

Three elements are key to our work:

1. *Empathy.* We are in constant contact with the children (and adults) we support, but also with the

people working with them on the ground at the frontline of this refugee crisis. We must be near them in order to address their evolving needs in the most suitable manner.

2. *The Creation of a positive community of support around these children.* Together as Europeans, we can be much more efficient in addressing this crisis. The HOME Project coordinates and forges effective partnerships between all relevant stakeholders, NGOs, private donors, corporations, media, public authorities, national and international organisations and foundations. We act as a solutions platform and a channel through which support can reach those with the most urgent needs.

3. *Efficiency and rapidity of operations.* Every minute, twelve refugee children are in the process of being displaced in the world. We are dealing with a very, very vulnerable population literally living on the edge. Every minute we lose with our backs to this problem takes a serious toll on human lives.

What would you do if bombs were falling right next to your house? Or if ISIS wanted to militarise your ten-year-old son? Or if the Taliban wanted to marry your eight-year-old daughter? What would you do?

I do not write to shock, disturb, or sadden. I simply want to ask people not to look away, not to look away and remain passive about the violence that is taking place on our doorsteps as Europeans. At the HOME Project, we not only provide a safe home, we give a voice to lone children, we make them feel visible and validated.

There is no more time to waste. We really are living this crisis. Supporting and empowering these children is a daily resistance to the violence committed against them. That is the promise we gave to Hamid. That is the promise we give every day to Omar, Amadou, to Ali, Osman, Bekir, Fariz, Mamadou, Diyar, Taha, and to all the children in our shelters.

These children could be our children. By turning our backs to them, it's like giving up on hope, giving up on love, giving up on a better world. In what kind of a world do we want to live? In what kind of a world do we want our children to live? These children are tomorrow's future.

Reflections on the Motive Power of Fire

Zsófia Bán

ON THE GELID NIGHT of 23 November 1823, Sadi Carnot awoke with a start. It was that dream again, one that had visited him for weeks now. By morning, he couldn't remember any of it and was left only with the feeling that it was that same one again. His body remembered; his mind was blank. He quivered and gasped, wanting so much to free himself from that stifling, haunting feeling, but he simply didn't know how. Outside, Paris lay in a stupor, and only the baker boys were stirring now, at two-thirty in the morning. Sadi's damp nightshirt clung to his spindly male frame. His gaunt body had never known a woman's touch, even now, at twenty-seven. Desire, however, surprised him every night, sweeping through him like a ravaging fire. Then, suddenly, it dawned on him: 'That was it,' he cried, 'that was my dream!' And as he said these words, the images began to flood over him, to rain down on him unrelentingly. Closing his eyes, petrified, Sadi wondered at those sharply focused images as they flitted by.

Sadi's full name was Nicolas Léonard Sadi Carnot, but everyone knew him as Sadi. As a young man, he had been

91

surprised – secretly irritated – that his father, the illustrious mathematician, brilliant engineer, intrepid leader of the Revolutionary Army, and member of the Directorate, should have chosen to name his son after a 13th-century Persian poet. Seriously? A Persian poet? Why not a general, why not a scholar or philosopher? What was it about this Persian, Sadi wondered, that had so impressed his father? He'd scoured his father's library and every nook and cranny of the Petit Palais, but found nothing of the Persian poet's works. Even the *Encyclopédie* offered no more than this: 'Twelfth-century Persian poet, called the Master of Speaking [this article is a stub].' What could he do? In the end, he'd made his peace with it. But when, at sixteen, he found himself at the École Polytechnique, on the first day of classes another kid let slip that secret name of his and people started calling him an Arab, which so infuriated Sadi that he – how to put it – smacked him one. Later he would be ashamed and make a ceremonious apology that earned him respect, albeit not a single friend. A patriot and child of the Revolution should be broad-minded and generous, thought scrawny little Sadi. From then on, the name stuck.

As the brutal sharpness of that furious fire's images began to fade, Sadi made a resolution on the spot. Hopping out of bed, he splashed his face with cold water from his Delft porcelain washbowl, towelled himself off, then went to his oak desk, covered in diagrams, calculations, and notes. He took a plume and paper, and quickly jotted down what he had seen in his dream. This is what he wrote:

'All eyes were raised to the top of the church. They beheld there an extraordinary sight. On the crest of the highest gallery, higher than the central rose window, there was a great flame rising between the two towers with whirlwinds of sparks, a vast, disordered, and furious flame, a tongue of which was borne into the smoke by the intermittent gusts of wind, from time to time. Below that fire, below the gloomy balustrade with its trefoils showing darkly against its glare, two spouts with monster throats were vomiting forth unceasingly that burning rain, whose silvery stream stood out against the shadows of the lower façade.

As they approached the earth, these two jets of liquid lead spread out in sheaves, like water springing from the thousand holes of a watering-pot. Above the flame, the enormous towers, two sides of which were visible in sharp outline, the one wholly black, the other wholly red, seemed still more vast with all the immensity of the shadow which they cast to the very sky.

Their innumerable sculptures of demons and dragons assumed a lugubrious aspect. The restless light of the flame made them move to the eye. There were griffins that seemed to be laughing, gargoyles which one fancied could be heard yelping, salamanders which puffed at the fire, tarasques which sneezed in the smoke. And among the monsters roused from their stony sleep by these flames, by this noise, there was one who walked about and could occasionally be seen passing by the glowing face of the pile, like a bat before a candle.

Here he was taken by a certain *frisson* and, feeling cold, he pulled his dressing gown around himself. He was seized by the feeling that this vision – but was it truly his vision at work here? – far from mollifying the horrific fire that haunted his dreams, was fanning it instead. What to make of the dream or its lingering effects? It was as if some force had emerged from the conflagration and heat, driving his quill over the page. He wrote as if moved by some mysterious energy – of which in turn he also wrote – then was overcome with horror. No, he shuddered, I cannot be doing this. No former student of the École Polytechnique, exponent of the practical sciences, could ever allow himself such a thing. It was madness. Or at least that is what they would surely call it later, when someone came to take him off and deposit him in some asylum. The Court's secret police, that's who it would be. They'd call it an obsession, a mania. They'd open a vein and set leeches on his body. Now he had to find some other way out, and fast. There must be some formula that would help him rein in this peculiar experience, while simultaneously preserving it and the energy and power he had gained. There must be something worthy of an engineer, son of a mathematician and revolutionary, something to stave off his immediate confinement to the madhouse (an unrelenting fear of his). Something to fit an invisible law into a properly scientific package, to make it visible. Some means by which to speak the truth about fire, light and heat being forces that move the world, neither madness nor sacrilege, but something driving the world, keeping it in motion. At this point, his horror and despair turned to tranquillity. Carefully he folded all those written thoughts in four, stamped them shut, and placed them in a small locked wooden box in his desk. Then he hid the tiny key in the desk's secret drawer. Finally, he took out a fresh sheet of paper and wrote the following:

Reflections on the Motive Power of Heat

To heat are due the vast movements which take place on the earth. Heat causes the agitations of the atmosphere, the ascension of clouds, the fall of rain and meteors, the currents of water which channel the

surface of the globe, and of which man has thus far
employed but a small portion. Even earthquakes and
volcanic eruptions are the result of heat.

Energy cannot be created (leave that to the Creator, thought
Sadi, who believed in Him, but barely). However, he continued
scrawling with determination, neither can energy be destroyed.
Hence no one can either gain or lose. Clear as day. But you
must know how to make do with what there is, with the
living force. Now this living force (*vis viva*), wrote Sadi, his
plume speeding now, can constantly take new forms, undergo
miraculous metamorphoses, flow from one place to another.
This, then, is the mysterious motive power – Sadi did not take
this to be matter – this energy (*energeia*) that does not die but
only transforms. Here he was gripped by unease. Who on
earth would publish this, or read it, or even take a single letter
of it seriously? In his mind's eye, he saw the works of his
fellow scientists on the bestseller lists, while his own little
book was ravaged by bookstore dust bunnies. But what
frightened him even more than failure was the chance he
would be charged with sacrilege, *lèse majesté*, witchcraft, or –
and this bothered him the most – insanity. Let's face it, the
Restoration was no friend to thought experiments and the
free flow of ideas. Would he not be discharged from the army
for good, his engineering career in ruins? Would his precise
and conscientious reports on the ramparts be entrusted to
another? What of the cartographical assignments so dear to his
heart? Would he – just a thought – be executed?

Ever since his father had been driven into exile, Sadi was
considered a mere reserve, on a two-thirds service pay. At this
point, he could entrust his young life to none but the
Sovereign (*Le Souverain!*) and his unbounded mercy. He could
not afford to take any risks. Now the images from his dream
came to life: he felt the scorching ardour of that savage,

rampant flame; saw the vast efforts, studies, expertise and poetry of centuries lurking in the burning edifice now exposed and flaming proudly. He saw its power crumble to nothing as he watched. *Eppur si muove!,* cried Sadi into the black and frosty night, in his surprisingly thin, almost waiflike voice, like a shrill battle cry. He took up his plume and resumed his train of thought: the sum total of energy within a given system is constant. Yes, thought Sadi triumphantly – *constant!* – settling down the moment he wrote the word. Loss, gain, defeat, victory; all leading to a balance, to equilibrium. What is more, continued Sadi, with no regard for any possible consequences, if two isolated systems come into contact, the energies of their thermal balances will stabilise, sooner or later. You just have to wait out the sooner-or-later, sit tight till that day comes. Until then – naturally – everything will get worse before it gets better (but – *shh!* – who guarantees it will get better?). For a while, you are run through the wringer, but someday everything will get back on track.

Sadi wrote without interruption until the following evening, then slept for two days like an exhausted log. He awoke to a loud, urgent knocking sound, a pounding. Terrified, Sadi was certain they had come to take him away in the black-curtained carriage. But there in the doorway stood his young writer friend who, dishevelled and sobbing, collapsed into his arms. He is dead, Sadi! Little Leopold is dead! Sadi accompanied Victor into the next room, sat him down in the large, winged armchair where he liked to read, brought him a glass of water, and watched him drink. There there, *mon ami*, there there, calm down. With a linen handkerchief, Victor wiped the tears rolling from his eyes and his ample Gallic nose. The kerchief bore a monogram: V. H.

As Victor spoke, Sadi quickly came to understand his recurring dream. Victor's firstborn, he said, was little Leopold, named after Victor's father, one of Napoleon's officers. He had suffered a burning fever for weeks, suspended between life and death. Victor now spoke in no more than a whisper, repeating, He died this evening. Sadi tried to console him, but where are cooling words to be found at such a time? Where the right formulas? He had met his young friend, now barely twenty, several years previously at the officers' casino that Victor frequented by association with his father. The six-year difference between them was of no consequence. Friendship, Life, Death – those were big words. And now, here, was one of them. But where was the force, the language for Death? Both men were still young and inexperienced. Sadi searched for words, thoughts, gestures. He sought the living force that can neither be created nor destroyed. And he embraced his broken friend. Yet there must be something more he could do, he thought. He resolved to tell Victor his recurring dream, the destruction of Notre Dame de Paris; finally, he understood exactly what that dream was all about. Clearly, Victor was quite moved as he looked at Sadi. Yet for Sadi, that was not enough. There must be more, he thought. Then he, too, in a whisper, told his friend: I wrote down my dream, the whole thing. If you like, I can read it to you. Victor nodded.

Sadi stood up, pulled shut the heavy brocade curtains, then walked to his desk, took the little key from the secret drawer, and removed the small carved wooden box where he had hidden the folded page. He broke the seal and read the dream to his friend. Victor drank in Sadi's words. The colour returned to his eyes. Victor pleaded: Give it to me, Sadi, if you know God, you will give it to me. Sadi did not know God, but he knew He existed. It would be nice to have some sort of formula for that, too, Sadi thought as he handed his dream to Victor, who slipped the folded page into the inner pocket of his coat, more or less over his heart. He took his hat. *Mon ami. Adieu.* Something along those lines. They embraced. Sadi watched him take his leave, and then all he saw was a bat flitting by his doorway.

As Sadi peers out the barred second-floor window of a yellow building, he is reminded of that evening eight years earlier, that farewell, that bat. In his letter, Victor promised to be here at five. Now it is four-thirty, but already pitch black. He has waited eight years for his friend to send word, and yet this half-hour is the hardest to bear. Then he spots the black carriage careering towards him along the tree-lined way. Sadi sees that Victor has a little trouble getting out (now the ample-bellied father of four, though not yet thirty), with a thick packet under his arm, tied up with string. '*Mon cher ami*,' wrote Victor, 'I finally bring you the manuscript of my novel, published this year. I entrust it to you in exchange for one passage. Keep it, with my gratitude. It will be safe here with you.' Victor is a star, the *enfant terrible* of French literature, Europe's *chouchou*. Everyone is reading Victor's books; no one reads Sadi's sole volume. On his door is written *Mania, Delirium, Caution*. What is not written: *Entropy, Thermodynamics, 2019, Cholera*.

Translated from the Hungarian by Jim Tucker

All of One Mind

Lisa Dwan

ON 13 APRIL 2001, I was fired from a shop job in London. It was Good Friday. In fairness, looking back, they were completely right. I was useless at it. I couldn't help myself from telling customers that garments were overpriced, poorly made or ill-fitting, and left the shop unattended every few minutes to have a cigarette. I was in one of life's troughs. I had only left Ireland a few months earlier, largely because a 'great man' of the theatre had told me in no uncertain terms: 'You'll never work in this town again.' At the time, in my youthful arrogance, I just laughed it off as a hilarious cliché, but I very quickly realised that he had the last laugh. Because he turned out rather quickly, in fact, to be right. I didn't really understand why. Actually, that's not true. I knew *why*. But *how* was this even possible? I didn't get how one man's narrative of me being 'tricky' could change the course of my life, causing me to leave the only home I'd ever known. Twenty years later, a certain hashtag trawled through that man's despicable 33-year-old reign and 'softened his cough'. They were braver women than me.

When I first moved to London, my father sent over a computer from Lidl, along with a digital skills course ('The European Computer Driving License') and a CD-ROM of 'Mavis Beacon Teaches Typing,' and off I went. 'You-are-doing-very-well. You-are-on-one-word-per-minute,' Mavis told me with as much computerised sincerity as she could muster. 'I can type!' I remember boasting to Fiona, an Irish customer who had come into the shop a couple of months before. As I was fastening her up, she told me that she ran a literary PR agency.

'Oh… what's PR?' I'd asked.

'Talking to people,' she said. 'You'd be good at it.' She mentioned some of her clients, described the books she publicised and was impressed that I'd read most of them. I was glad she didn't buy that awful jacket with the weird zips. I liked her.

'Wetting rain,' as my mother would have called it, melded with my own tears as I fled from the threshold of that shop's awning where I had just been fired. I had no education, no family, no prospects – my fairytale dream of becoming an actress was slipping further and further away. I couldn't even hold down a shop job. How was I going to pay rent? How could I call my parents over Easter and tell them I'd been fired? I had fallen from conventional safety into one of life's little cracks, and most of all, I had this funny little accent. I felt the weight of all my failures as I sat on a pew in St Dominic's Priory, sheltering from the lashing rain.

The priory was on the bend between South End Green and Camden. I don't know what possessed me to run in there, or how long I stayed. I wept into my hair and my hands until eventually, a man sidled over to me.

'Do you want me to hear your confession?' he asked.

I hadn't been in a confessional box since I was 12 years old. Uncertain, in case they were going to send me back out into the rain again, I whispered, 'I'm very lapsed. I can't even remember how the prayers go.'

'That's okay,' he said. 'Give it a go. You might be surprised by what you remember.'

'Bless me, Father, for I have... *fuck*... oh sorry... *shit*... sorry!'

'Just tell me your sins,' he said, and I replied with sobs, snot and confusion. He was right after all, because suddenly the same old prefabricated list came flooding back with all of its solemn insincerity: 'I was disrespectful to my mother; I said a bad word...' He seemed pleased.

He asked me what my favourite piece of music was.

'Bach's cello concerto,' I answered.

'Well, for your penance, go home and listen to that,' he said. 'I'm Derek, by the way. You'll find me here most days.'

Derek was no priest.

When I stepped back outside, I turned on my Samsung flip phone and there was one new voicemail: 'Hello Lisa. This is Fiona. We met in a shop on Hampstead High Street. Look, for some reason, I like you, and if you would be interested in a job in publishing, give me a call.' I phoned her back immediately and told her that *fortuitously*, as it just so happened, I had a gap in my diary.

'There's an Irish client none of us wants to handle,' she told me when we met. After a pause, her voice lowered. 'He's from the North, and... if you're happy for me to throw you in at the deep end, and give it a go, there might be a proper job at the end of it for you.'

I had never been to Northern Ireland. I'm from a small town in the middle of Ireland, between Dublin and Galway. We were brought up violently apathetic towards the North. Questions about Ireland's civil war, the IRA and The Troubles were – much like drink driving, or the plausibility of the Eucharist – frowned upon in our house and met with terse, taciturn responses.

In truth, anyone who had heard Gordon Wilson's testimony about holding his dying daughter's hand under the rubble of 1987's Enniskillen bombing would understand any parent's desire to turn that horror and helplessness into hope; the urgency to pull a child's imagination away from the graves, the bloodshed and the stories of our history, guiding them towards a broader landscape, to another possibility. And that, to us at least, was Europe.

My parents may have often taken a somewhat questionable 'free-range' approach to parenting, but on this point, their efforts stuck out. We understood that they were born to children of 'New Ireland', born out of the bitter bloodshed of a civil war, and they were determined not to let that define us. I don't ever remember seeing a tricolour at home. Instead, our house is called 'Shalom' and is cluttered with Spanish Dolls, Harry Belafonte and Miriam Makeba records, and pictures of Italian tenors line our walls, alongside Padro Pio's glove and various African carvings. There were stories told to us about our family history, that the Dwan's were black Irish – either Italian, Spanish or Portuguese depending on who was telling it – and that they'd arrived onto the shores of Ireland with the Armada. Who knows what the truth is, but our name does translate into Gaelic as 'Ó Dubháin': the black one.

'Falls Road, please,' I said to the black cab driver at Belfast Airport. The only thing he batted an eyelid at, quite rightly, was my low-cut top and inappropriate cleavage. I had spent the previous night trying to apply my Mavis Beacon know-how to a press release for a book I hadn't even read and didn't have time to buy any 'professional' attire. In desperation, I called my sister, who is in international relations.

'Help me,' I begged. 'Tell me what to say. I've never even seen a press release let alone written one!'

'Jesus Christ, Lisa – you cannot do this, it's insane!'

'I have to,' I whimpered, 'it's my only chance of a job.' There was silence on the other end of the line, until eventually, she said, 'Well, I suppose you could call him a political visionary.' P-O-L-I-T-I-C-A-L (spacebar) V-I-S-I-O-N-A-R-Y. I was off.

In late 2001, a new term entered our collective consciousness: WAR ON TERROR. It was the phrase of the moment. Bush and Blair bandied it about *ad nauseam*, but I soon learned that one man's terrorist is another failed actress's new PR client. Enter Gerry Adams.

The fact that our introduction began with him correcting the name of his book on my press release was indicative of our future together. In fact, I turned out to be so terribly bad at my job that at times I was somehow brilliant. Looking back, I didn't know what any of the rules were so I broke them all, and that tends to get attention.

Gerry Adams was the only terrorist I'd ever heard of, and for any child growing up in England or Ireland, his was a face, and voice, to be feared. Margaret Thatcher even had the bizarre notion of banning his voice from being broadcast, which, incidentally, is how Stephen Rea – the great Beckett actor – paid off his mortgage: by portraying Adams' voice on radio and television in the late 1980s.

Overnight I found myself chairing press conferences in the House of Commons, with a room full of hostile political journalists. 'Ah, lads, please. Can we talk about the book?'

'Not so long ago, she would have been arrested for knowing me,' Gerry once told a young British journalist. 'I may have been better off!' I retorted, 'So might I!' he joked.

While the War on Terror raged, I listened to personal testimonies of waterboarding, internment and even young blindfolded men being taken up in helicopters and pushed out – not knowing they were only a few feet off the ground until they landed. I heard about Belfast, Falls Road, prison, hunger strikes, about the long road to the peace process. I remember a long car journey in which I asked Gerry if he resented me for my apathy; for the privilege that allowed me to be so ambivalent about something he devoted his life to. Did he resent me for the perspective Europe gave me? He understood when I said that it would be inauthentic for me to foster sentimental feelings about the North. We swapped stories, told jokes, he recited poetry. He forgave me whenever I was late, or gave him the wrong information, or turned up too hungover to function. I watched him laugh, hug trees. I saw him vulnerable. He was there the day my heart was broken. He saw me get sober and pull my life together. He rang when my dad slipped into a coma. He turned up at the opening night of my Beckett trilogy in Belfast.

The last time I met Gerry Adams was in the gardens of Leinster House, our DAIL or government buildings. He had invited me to watch the historic abortion bill being sworn in, from the gallery. I was in Dublin performing a one-woman show from my own adaptation of Beckett's prose. He had attended the night before and told me that he found it very moving but didn't understand it. I told him Beckett often wanted his work to play on the nerves of the audience, not their intellect. These 'texts for nothing' were written in the 1950s when Europe was trying to come to terms with herself after the war, as she is again now. I called the piece 'No's Knife' from a line in the piece: 'The screaming silence of No's knife in Yes's wound.'

It was intimidating territory, attempting to turn a gathering of Beckett's prose into a theatrical piece. What was I going to do with my body? One phrase gave me the greatest visual clue: *'I AM DOWN IN THE HOLE THE CENTURIES HAD DUG... centuries of filthy weather... flat on my face in the dark with the creeping saffron waters it slowly drinks.'*

I'm from the Bog, the centre of Ireland, where the Bog of Allen lies across it like an open wound. Where 'the creeping saffron waters' contain a set of chemicals that preserves flesh. I thought of the bog bodies that were dug up from the ground, centuries-old, hands bound – a brutal death. The same creatures that inspired Heaney to write *Tollund Man*. The bog where the IRA discarded bodies. I thought of bodies that lay across fields in Flanders. I thought about our unburied dead. The wounds that won't die. The traumas that won't shush.

Gerry asked me if I wouldn't mind sending him a recording of some of the Beckett pieces so he could play them to a friend of his who was dying.

'Leave! All you had to do was stay at home... Home! They wanted me to go home... Where would I go if I could go? Who would I be if I could be? What would I say if I had a voice?'

You'd be hard-pressed not to hear all the political resonances in these words. As I read and rehearsed, the lines' images flashed before me; all the drowned unnamed refugee souls. I thought of that image of that little boy, Alan Kurdi, washed up on a shore in Turkey. Who would he have been if he had been allowed to be? I think of all the women who are still 'down in the hole the centuries have dug.' I think of the remains of the 800 or so babies recently found in the septic tank of the Magdalene laundry, ten miles from where I grew up and wonder what they would say if they had a voice? I think of Lyra McKee, the young 29-year-old journalist from Northern Ireland who had been shot and killed in Derry in 2019, the most recent casualty in a conflict that has left more than 3,000 people dead. I think again of 'the screaming silence of No's knife in Yes's wound.'

So much of Beckett is communing with the dead. And in a way, I feel the presence, the voices of all that lot with me. Or, as Beckett says, 'those of the dead, those of the living and those of those who are not yet born... It is they have thought me all I know.' They're my guides up there under the lights, watching on in the darkness.

One of the greatest gifts from my 13 years or so of sensory deprivation in his *Not I* – a play for a disembodied pair of lips – was that as time went on, I increasingly stopped feeling like a human being. Hovering eight feet above the stage with my blindfolded head tied into a vice, my arms in brackets, was ultimately just so damn liberating. To have your body removed, as a woman, was one of the greatest gifts I've ever known. I got to play a consciousness – a trillion voices – not one consciousness but consciousness itself, a continent of consciousness. It actually altered my voice, and a shocking guttural tone arrived from way beyond my female or even human register. I got to peel away the trappings and entrapment of a woman, of what society has done to us as women, go beyond the limitations we set ourselves, the little palatable realities shaped by our fears.

The truths Beckett tells, and the picture of us he puts before us, strip away false comforts. Beckett has shown me time and again that sentimentality isn't truthful – it is the language of gangsters. Beckett offers no history lesson, no sermon, no story, only the *wound*.

It concerns me deeply that we live in times when new boundary lines are being drawn. When the news is filled with the same old conversations about nationalism that never took us anywhere; when even swastikas rear their depraved heads again; when Ireland faces the potential of having a new hard border driven back through her heart; when masked men shoot dead a bright star in her prime and parade down the O'Connell Street in Dublin. In a world being led by the likes of Trump and Putin, forging division, perpetuating hate and fear and lies, against the backdrop of Brexit and the rise of nationalism throughout Europe and the world. We need a different narrative, to overcome the oppressive voices that threaten us from without and from within.

In the world Beckett showed me, I have learned to give my imagination permission to dissolve the boundaries of my small self, where, on this stage, I go beyond the confines of identity that imprison me – it is here that I find this new narrative, this new tale of myself.

We need to see that we are much greater and richer than our paltry ideas of identity can stretch to, that we are, as Beckett says, 'Of one mind, all of one mind... deep down we're fond of one another.'

No Science,
No Future

Silvia Bencivelli

I GREW UP IN ITALY in the eighties: in those days, my country
was flourishing and full of optimism. We were coming out of
a period of high social tension and becoming a modern
country. Employment, education, health, and family law were
at the centre of major reforms, albeit at the cost of growing
public debt. And we could finally hold our heads high in
Europe. Even our football team was doing well!

My parents were scientists (my mother a doctor; my father
a university researcher) and they were both working in the
public sector. They had permanent jobs, meaning that they
were much better off than their parents had been at the same
age, and they weren't afraid of the future. No-one was.

Europe was leading the world – economically,
technologically and culturally. We had been living in peace for
at least three decades and it seemed that things could only get
better.

We were reaping the benefits of Europe's rich history.
Research and intellectual exchange had made our small
continent a hotbed of innovation and culture, and after two
world wars, we seemed to have understood that the best

future is one we build together. At the time, my family lived in one of these great centres of exchange: Pisa. Historically, it has always been a city of science, and today it is the site of three state universities, all of which are among the best in Italy, according to national and international rankings. Over the years, it has established a strong, cohesive, cutting-edge scientific community, one that helped establish Italian computer science in the 1960s, linking it to ideals of collectivism and progress, and one which was responsible for some of the most important scientific discoveries in the world. But most notably, Pisa was the birthplace of Fibonacci, the inspiration behind the rebirth of European mathematics in the Middle Ages, and of Galileo Galilei, who alongside Nicolaus Copernicus (Polish), Isaac Newton (English), René Descartes (French) and many of our continent's other illustrious sons, led what is known as the Scientific Revolution. There was a lot to be proud of.

I was a teenager in Italy in the nineties. The start of the decade saw the fall of the Berlin Wall and the signing of the Maastricht Treaty in 1992. I remember my French pen pal's older brother coming home from a holiday in Germany with a piece of coloured concrete. And I remember a funny little song that was played on Italian radio at the time, which went 'I'm packing my bags and I'm off to Maastricht!' In those days, I was studying French and German at school, and playing the violin in a classical youth orchestra. Every summer I went camping with my family in France, Spain, England, Scotland, Germany, Denmark, Holland… It was fun: we were safe, rich, free. And Europe was our home.

Back then, Italy considered itself to be a modern country, perfectly in line with other European nations, but a country discovering that it was founded on massive corruption. The result was a quick and dramatic change in traditional politics, but also the start of twenty years of Berlusconi governments. At the same time, we were becoming a country of mass immigration, particularly from Eastern Europe. We were starting to guard our riches jealously, and were experiencing a resurgence of racism and fascism. For the first time in our history, the birth to death ratio was negative: a modern country, as we all know, does not have children.

Meanwhile, I was becoming an adult. I went to a university with a 600-year history, Italy's finest scientific institution. While I was studying there, just a few kilometres from my house, the largest research centre in the country was built, alongside the first gravitational-wave observatory in Europe. Our European friends could still make fun of us for having a premier with little regard for institutional formalities (to say the least), but when it came to science and culture, we were still strong and proud, and rightly so.

Then, almost imperceptibly, things changed. In my family and all around us.

My brother moved to Beijing and lived there for four years: his three children now speak Italian and Chinese, and not a word of French, German or Spanish. I began a career in communications and have been freelance ever since: I've never had a permanent job and I'm not sure I ever will. Italy is still a rich country, but it has come to think of itself as poor and stopped growing. We are rediscovering ourselves as nationalists, we have put our government in the hands of a nationalist party. We are also losing our ties with Europe. And Europe itself is losing its composure for fear of losing its identity, whatever that may mean. We are in danger of burying our peace under an avalanche of petty, short-sighted selfishness. But what's worse is that we're ruining our future. I see it from the observatory that is scientific research, which in Italy – more so than in the rest of Europe – is losing out on recognition, prestige and funding.

My country, in particular, seems to have stopped believing in culture, and science in particular: we are no longer investing in science and culture, and young people are no longer encouraged to become ambitious researchers for the good of humanity. Over the last ten years, public investment in research and development has dropped by over 20 per cent. In absolute terms, today we are investing (between public and private) a little over 20 billion euros per year, which is less than half that invested by France, and even more pitiful when compared to Germany. These days, the percentage of GDP dedicated to research in Italy is little over 1 per cent. In France, we're talking about 2.2 per cent and in Germany 2.8 per cent. Now, the Spanish have also overtaken us.

To put it another way, we are the eighth largest economy in the world, or perhaps the ninth, but we are twenty-seventh in terms of investment in research and thirty-fifth for the number of researchers by population. This is the start of a decline that will be hard to reverse. One that is demonstrated by just how many scientists are leaving us and emigrating to other European countries, to the United States, and increasingly in recent years to Asia: around 30,000 in a decade, estimates suggest.

To complete the picture, even the city of Pisa – for centuries so open to exchange with the entire Mediterranean – is presently governed by a nationalist party that is blocking the arrival of foreigners and cutting cultural funding. And my fellow citizens voted them in.

It is absurd to find yourself in this position, hoping that other European countries will not follow in our footsteps. And that, in the hope of a quick U-turn in Italian politics, Europe will stay strong and look to a future that cannot be built without a culture of science.

My proposal for restoring hope in a more optimistic Europe is, in the meantime, to go back to the beginning. To teach our children differently, whilst still instilling curiosity and pride in being European.

I would suggest that we teach them history, geography and languages from all over the planet, not just our continent. We need to make children understand that here, today, our lives are much easier than in many places around the world. However, we shouldn't be complacent or see this as our 'reward'. Instead, it is a duty for them and for the previous generation to defend our shared European history and cultural roots; roots that have blossomed thanks to influences from the rest of the world. Just as Fibonacci did in the 13th century, when he popularised Arabic arithmetic across the Western World.

Because it's no longer enough to try to get to know your neighbour: we can't keep taking for granted our cultural, scientific or even economic position. And the only way we can achieve this is by continuing to be open to interactions with others in order to experience mutual enrichment.

Lastly, and more pragmatically, I think there is an urgent need to talk to adults of my generation. Investing in the future means doing what we've done in the past: focusing on science and research, encouraging young people to ask questions and spend their lives studying the answers, putting them in a position to do so without having to make sacrifices.

Nowadays, Italian children know that it will be hard to make a living as a scientific researcher: study grants have reduced and funding bodies now reward perseverance and loyalty to those in charge over merit. Some areas are still functioning very well: blue-sky research in physics, cosmology and certain sectors of biology – in no small part thanks to European grants such as those bearing the ERC stamp. But for many other young scientists, staying at university or finding a public research post is a dream, and anyone who does manage to make it happen knows immediately that it will mean living on low wages, with no job security or guaranteed funding. Only the most stubborn will survive, those with fewer family ties who can leave their hometown more easily, and those with the greatest financial privilege. Unfortunately, that tends to mean that those who survive are ambitious men, with strong families behind them. This also results in universities being ever more elitist and dominated by the usual suspects, with the only real prospect of change to be found on happy islands of outstanding research.

Underfunded science that excludes marginalised individuals is also a science that struggles to make itself useful and to listen to the needs of the wider community. Yet we have an urgent need for science, especially in the field of ecology, and a huge responsibility as Europeans. We were the first to exploit the planet's resources, and to pollute it with no thought for the future. But climate knows no borders. Now it's up to us to be the first to propose solutions that give everyone on Earth the same opportunities to grow and to be happy that we experienced and created for ourselves. And these same opportunities must be guaranteed, immediately, for future generations. What is at stake here is not only peace for us in Europe, but peace for the entire planet.

Translated from the Italian by Ruth Clarke

The Bull's Bride

Nora Ikstena

THE HORIZON STRETCHING ACROSS the sea was changeful; one evening shrouded in a tender mist, the next it would disappear in a haze of clouds. On yet another, it drew a thin, sharp boundary line across a clear, bright sky. That night the wind was subtle and mild. Nonetheless, leaves stirred in it, clouds moved, and waves rushed ashore.

The path of the setting sun on the sea expanded from a narrow streak into endless glittering water, and the light created a shifting play of shadows, which raced across the earth without touching it.

Birds flitting about above the treetops stilled their wings now and then, surrendering to the wind. The morning air was fresh and brisk and replete with creature sounds, but the evening air, in which a flittermouse quietly cut circles, was like velvet. The meadow by the sea had burst into blossom.

Europa was picking flowers in the meadow. In a light, white linen dress, barefoot, she had escaped for a brief respite from the harsh authority of her father's house. Here everything was different. Sensing her true nature, she seemingly abandoned herself to the wide and open expanse. She felt as if she was herself a meadow flower – camomile, wild angelica, lamb's ear. She could not imagine what was to come – maybe a beast

115

would crush her underfoot, a scythe mow her down, or a human pluck her, perhaps braid her into a wreath. Or maybe she would just wilt beautifully.

Europa lay down in the meadow where a gentle drowsiness overcame her young, lovely body.

In a dream, she saw a bright nocturnal sky, stars that had assembled in a circle. But the circle broke and the stars scattered helter-skelter across the dark vault of the sky. Then she heard what sounded like a beast's heavy moan. She gazed around and saw under the star-lit sky a gigantic white bull lying on the black earth. One of his front legs was badly injured and streaming blood, which the bull was licking. She plucked up her courage and, in the dream as if in reality, she approached the bull, the enormous beast – so large and so helpless in his pain. Europa lifted his injured foreleg, tore up her linen dress and bandaged the bull's wound. She caressed his massive head until he drifted off to sleep.

When Europa awoke in the flowering meadow, she gazed at the sky and images slid across her eyes – floods of sin in which she did not perish, walls that did not hold her back, a cross she did not bear, a confessional tree whose fruit she did not pluck, an altar at which she made no pledge, a sacrificial shrine where she made no sacrifice. She was but a tiny flower in a meadow by the sea, and yet she was part of all living things.

It was time to head home, where work and her stern father awaited her. She waded through the meadow thinking about the enormous white bull and how, in her dream, which had been as real as if she were awake, she had managed to bandage his wound.

She was not the kind of daughter her father had hoped for – though obedient, respectful, pious, she would on occasion demonstrate the deviousness of a woman. As much as she could, she respected and loved her mighty father. She knew that he was a capable ruler but also that he would at some point sell his own flesh-and-blood.

Whenever she could, Europa escaped her father's clutches by running off to the seaside meadow or the cattle barn. In the barn's hayloft, she found a nook to hide in, a tiny locked room with a key in the door. From it dangled a pendant – a white dove. She took the key and slipped it into a dress pocket near her heart. Then, in her hideaway, she would read, entering a world without hostility or betrayal, where one's conscience could not be bought, where believers of other faiths and differing opinions were not killed, where one's word was honourable and the word 'honour' itself had value, where love and loyalty prevailed over hypocrisy and lies. Europa was fully aware that all the truths and wisdom she gained from her reading drove a wedge between her and her father, and worse still elicited anger and hate from him.

Returning from the meadow, Europa was met by an agitated maid. Where had she wandered off to for so long? A very influential suitor had arrived to see her father and ask for Europa's hand in marriage. She must wash quickly, anoint herself with sweet perfume, don her splendid parade dress and put on her silk shoes. What a sight her bare, filthy feet, the maid complained. And just look at her tangled hair, her creased and torn linen dress. She looked like a ragamuffin, only missing a beggar's alms bag. My God, the maid wailed, if your father could see you. If only he could see you now. As she grabbed the disobedient daughter's hand, her freshly-picked meadow flowers fell scattered across the marble tiles. Europa was back in her father's coercive and authoritarian world.

The maid took pains to wash and scrub Europa down, she brushed and curled her hair, laced her body into a restrictive corset, pulled on her parade dress, and made up her face, white and inaccessible.

Thus embellished, Europa stood mute and stock-still before the large, gilded mirror, gazing at the maid's carefully created but unreal image. The silk shoes would make her feet smart from blisters. Her linen dress lay discarded by the scented bath. Taking the key with the white-dove pendant from the special pocket of the linen frock and grasping it tightly in her fist, she was now ready to face her father's might.

Her father had taken care of everything. A purple carpet ran the full length of the long corridor, as far as the grand hall. Vases were filled with lilies, which Europa associated with the smell of death, not life. She stopped for a moment and looked up. She had never before thought of looking up in this place, but now she could see that decorating the dark blue ceiling was the same circle of stars from her dream in the seaside meadow, the circle that had broken and the stars that had scattered across the sky.

People in parade uniforms crowded the hall, giving her curious looks and hypocritical smiles. There were rulers, their subordinates, diplomats and religious leaders. From wisdom gained in her hideaway, Europa was aware of her power, but still, she trembled wondering what was happening behind the scenes, because no one knew who would stab whom in the back. Nonetheless, they all had the same unshakeable ally – religion and God, the One and Only, who would save any lost lambs.

Europa walked through this pack of wolves, clutching ever more tightly her hideaway key and pendant. Here was a kingdom by appearances, while the truth lay in her hiding place, behind the hay stored in the barn.

To her father's right stood the influential suitor. Her father took Europa's hand and led her to her intended, saying to him: 'Look, here is my ode to joy.'

Lanterns were lit, fanfares sounded, and the festivities began. Europa obediently waltzed with her father's chosen suitor. Increasingly, however, she found herself unable to breathe. She asked for permission to go out onto the large balcony, for a breath of fresh air.

From the beautiful, manicured gardens, a slight breeze wafted in the scent of cypresses and earth. Europa gazed at the sky and the same images slid past her eyes again – floods of sin in which she did not perish, walls that did not hold her back, a cross she did not bear, a confessional tree whose fruit she did not pluck, an altar where she made no pledge, a sacrificial shrine where she made no sacrifice.

She had never been beyond the castle and these garden walls; even the meadow by the sea was fenced in from the world outside.

Europa stood on the balcony, listening to the rabble behind her in the grand hall – the hypocrites had let down their defences and were now indulging in cheap jokes about the people who lived beyond those fortified walls.

And suddenly, not in a dream now but in reality, Europa witnessed a miraculous vision. Cutting through the cypresses, the white bull approached the balcony. Billows of breath blew from his nostrils into the brisk air and in the semi-darkness his golden horns glittered. He came right up to Europa, leaned his large head against the balcony railing and gazed at her with submissive, inviting eyes, which seemed to say, 'Come, let's flee from this place.'

Her father had anxiously hurried out to the balcony, but on seeing the bull he froze. Helplessly he watched as Europa climbed onto the bull's back. She reached out her hand to her father. In her nervousness, she had stretched out her left hand, which held the key. In a rage, her father grabbed it and tore it from the white-dove pendant, which remained in Europa's grasp as she and the bull retreated from the balcony.

The bull jumped over the fortified wall and they galloped away. Now, for the first time, Europa's eyes witnessed reality. People chained together, very much like the circle of stars in the sky, were all living their own lives. They spoke different languages in both a literal and figurative sense. Poor huts alternated with magnificent castles. The foremost thieves were given honourable positions while petty crooks were thrown in jail. Ministers and priests confessed horrifying sins. Fear plagued the cities, fear of revenge seekers, who would kill not the guilty but the innocent. Mobs spilt out onto the streets. They demanded self-determination, they fought for their rights to sing their own songs, to eat their own bread and drink their own water. They told the truth – the one that she had sensed in her hideaway in the barn, the one that had long ago been forgotten by those in their vanity fair parade clothes, the truth in Europa's head that had so angered her father. They galloped on and saw the vast seas full of overcrowded boats, where people who looked different and were clearly in despair fought for survival, hoping to make it to shore. So profound was their despair that they were ready to throw their own people overboard. They galloped on and saw on the shore the many bodies that had been lost at sea and heavy trucks full of dead souls. As they journeyed further, they also saw hideaways where people gathered to read books, listen to music, and admire paintings. But these refuges, and those who populated them, were far too few.

Mounted on the bull's back, Europa stared wide-eyed at it all – a staggering voyage through reality, so beautiful and yet so heart-rending at once.

How long had they been charging along like that? The bull stopped by the seashore. It was a totally different sea from the small, fenced-in strip of Europa's father's home. Free and vast, with an unreachable horizon and a high, bright blue sky above its transparent waters.

After his long journey, the bull drank greedily. He looked

at Europa for a moment with almost human eyes and then, exhausted, fell asleep.

Europa threw off her restrictive parade dress and waded naked into the sea. In her left fist, she still held the white-dove pendant from the key that had remained in her father's hand. Europa knew one day she would return to retrieve the key from the might of her father.

Translated from the Latvian by Margita Gailitis
Co-edited by Vija Kostoff

Change Is Not Just a Hashtag

Žydrūnė Vitaitė

LATELY, I HAVE BEEN taking pleasure in boundaries – the change from one year to another, winter to spring – and I'm even beginning to warm to birthdays simply because the crossing of a border (of age, date or understanding) is a perfect time to think about one's life and reflect, to have deeper conversations and, certainly, to grow.

Some of the most interesting conversations I have had about boundaries have been with my grandmother. Born in 1929, she will soon celebrate her 90th birthday. That is perhaps why our discussions have long since moved away from everyday life, whether we want them to or not, and delved much deeper. There was one weekend when my usual question to her, 'How are you?' opened up a lot more. 'You know, I'm living the happiest years of my life,' said my 89-year-old grandmother with such enthusiasm and conviction that there was no way I could doubt it. 'I have never had more freedom than I do now. I finally have time to listen to the birds, to observe how nature changes with the seasons, and to be at peace with my own future. When I look back on my life, there were so many things that I was afraid to talk about. I lived through war, through German and Soviet invasions, and occupation; I washed the bloody clothes of my tortured brother, said goodbye to people I knew who were sent to the gulag; I scoured ruins and rubble searching for loved ones; I endured the nationalisation of private property; I lived through family dramas and nationwide instability as Lithuania regained its independence. There were so many moments of both pain and happiness, but never in my life were there better years than in my old age. I now feel good and at peace with the future.'

This conversation only lasted for a few hours, but I have carried it with me for a long time. I had never heard of people being more content in their old age than in their youth. So what does a person need in order to be happy? What is happiness? Can we be 90-something and, having seen so many painful things in life, still believe in the future? Or maybe it is this belief in the future, while living in the present, that allows us to breathe freely and experience happiness.

I was born in 1988. Freedom is a word that came to define my generation, one that I carry with me consciously and proudly, believing it to be a pure and undeniable truth. The following year, in August 1989, three Baltic nations – Lithuania, Latvia and Estonia – held a peaceful demonstration in which two million people, without the help of social media or a hashtag, gathered together and formed a 650km human chain in order to call for their nations' independence. This demonstration showed how important every individual contribution is to the collective, and how powerful it can be to unite and take part. Such conscious steps in the name of freedom are of great importance to me, although I often experience these freedoms without thinking of how they were fought for by generations before me. With the thirtieth anniversary of the Baltic Way, the symbolic meaning of the human chain and its contribution to historic changes cannot be denied.

Lithuania, though a young democracy, would not be where it is now if not for the willingness of young people to get involved in creating change. For example, the year 2012 saw the birth of 'The White Gloves', a movement that seeks to empower young people to become active citizens, to fight political corruption and monitor elections. Similarly, the 'Let's Do It' campaign brings together over two hundred thousand people each year to clean up and conserve the environment on a national level, and has since become 'Let's Do It World', taking place in over one hundred countries. These are just some examples of how socially active young people in Lithuania are helping to build a better future and are working together for the good of the community. At times, it seems that I live in the land of my dreams, but is that really so?

In the summer of 2016, I received a message from a US professor I know, Thomas Andrew Bryan, about a Syrian refugee called Redwan, a young and promising journalist who was fluent in English. He was keen to build a new life for himself in Lithuania – a country that, to a refugee from war-torn Syria, was filled with promise. At that time, the issue of refugees in Lithuania was controversial. Nevertheless, the majority of the country's educated population were keen to make a bold statement about it, to lead by example and show how officials should take action, what to say and what not to say, and how Lithuania should deal with this situation in a modern way. So, that same summer, I asked around for help on Redwan's behalf, approaching those I knew to have been outspoken in their support for refugee resettlement – help in finding a place to live, in navigating the system, in simply spending time with him in town. To my surprise, the most passionate and demagogic advocates for social justice couldn't even find the time to have a coffee with him. Help began and ended with a few posts on social media, and my plan to put Redwan up for two weeks quickly turned into eight weeks.

Those two months proved to me that change is not brought about by a few 'likes' and shares online. Change requires much more. Change sometimes requires that you unconditionally 'rent out' your sofa, and incessantly make phone calls trying to convince other people that Syrians are people too. Change requires understanding that certain intelligent and influential friends will do exactly nothing to help give someone a second chance in life, even when that person is standing right in front of them. It was a great lesson for me, showing that we constantly need to test the limits of our social bubbles, to ask ourselves how much our own actions are about maintaining an image, or making our world – by our own example – a better place.

Digital activism has achieved quite a lot: it has empowered society to organise, mobilise, unite and to bring difficult questions out into the open – from the Arab Spring to the #WomensMarch, #HeForShe campaigns, or the record-breaking #ASLIceBucketChallenge. Technology allows us to raise awareness about things. On the other hand, together with the rise in popularity of digital activism, real activism can be buried in a like and re-share cemetery, while real carriers of change fail to be reflected in ratings or the numbers of followers, or even in ordinary gratitude. The border between change in the digital world and real change in society is still quite slippery.

'It is very hard to change things, but worth the effort,' said Lithuanian businesswoman D. Grigienė to me once. And the best proof of how hard, and worthwhile, it is when you try to make such a change in your own life. I'm not speaking about starting to work out, hiking a hundred kilometres, or sleeping in a forest in -18 C (all of which I've tried and all of which is possible!). To understand what you want to change, and to make that change in your own life in order to live happily – that is a kind of great magic, as well as a very long marathon to run.

When, in 2011, I finished my degree in economics and jumped straight into the telecommunications industry, there were only a few women working in the sector. I was finding it difficult introducing myself to clients, I had no idea what my strengths were, or how to stop admonishing myself for every mistake I made in meetings. When my own sister – the first woman hired as a design engineer in a construction company in Lithuania – asked me for advice about how to ensure that she would be respected, I simply could not understand why these kinds of questions were still being asked in the 21st century. Out of these shared experiences, and the timely arrival of like-minded people, the first Lithuanian women's mentoring program was born: Women Go Tech. And only after interviewing several hundred women for the program, all with very similar questions, did I begin to realise how important it is to create long-lasting change. And not just a hashtag.

The several hundred women that signed up for Women Go Tech have taught me a lot about myself and also society at large. It taught me how restrictive gender stereotypes can be, how women often lack self-belief and courage, and struggle to put themselves first. At the same time, my experience with these women has inspired me, demonstrating what can happen when those fears and insecurities are overcome, and real change occurs. I witnessed former dentists becoming programmers, mothers with several children going back to work as tech project leaders, philologists becoming engineers, women who – after one meeting with a mentor – decided to change their lives.

These women, who didn't know what they wanted, have now found purpose and genuine freedom within this industry to create, without fear of discrimination. Change requires patience and perseverance. Hashtags aren't enough to bring about change because technology is only powerful when a human being is beneath it – one with their own history, feelings, vulnerabilities and power to transform.

The process of bringing women into technology in Lithuania is a symbol to me of that great power we call 'freedom'. Freedom to understand oneself, to choose one's own way. Freedom to try, to fail, to accept oneself in both failure and success. Only with the freedom to be yourself can you accept the Other – by growing, creating, failing, and rising again. Only with the freedom to create can I grow as a person and as a member of a community.

I return again and again to my grandmother's words: 'I have never had more freedom than I do now.' We are separated by more than half a century, but in repeating her words I slowly begin to feel them take root inside of me. Thanks to the patience and constant struggle of my ancestors, I live in a country where the word freedom, although fragile, is now guaranteed. I live in a time where I can choose whether to listen to the news or the birds. I live at peace with the thought that if I listen to what my inner self says about the road forward, I will be able to follow it.

At the same time, I live in a time when I am responsible for the fact that my choices can allow that freedom to blossom. My choices can tear down stereotypes, allowing me to better myself, my community, my country, and my Europe. Today, I am happy and thankful for the freedom to create, and I dream that my fellow Europeans, including the refugee Redwan, will see enough light to be able to believe in the future. I feel responsible for not only upholding the freedom that my grandmother so enjoys, but to make it even stronger, more robust, so that in my old age I can also say, 'I am living the happiest years of my life.'

Today I know one thing: it begins and ends inside of me.

Translated from the Lithuanian by Rimas Uzgiris

Remote Control

Carine Krecké

Characters:
SUPERVISOR (female)
REGULATOR (male)
PARLIAMENTARIAN (male)

Setting:
MEETING ROOM

The three protagonists are seated motionless around a U-shape table with open space in the middle. A clock on the wall strikes 3 p.m.

SUPERVISOR: (*Speaks fast with a high-pitched voice and German accent, without looking at the other protagonists*) Trilogue on High Standards of Supervisory Surveillance, sixteenth round, as prerequisite to the 2021 Autumn Package of the Interinstitutional Regulatory Convergence Board, kick-starting the nine hundred thousand and eleven core guidelines of the Too-Big-To-Fail-Versus-Too-Big-To-Regulate Rulebook. Good afternoon.

(*REGULATOR and PARLIAMENTARIAN give SUPERVISOR a brief nod*)

HSSS trilogues are operational on a High-Level Paying, I mean, Playing Field (*starts to frantically sort a stack of paper*), thanks to robust multi-task decision-making based on fear, sorry, *peer* comparisons and in-depth transversal analyses of risk-sensitive data gathered on a wide scale (*continues organising papers while talking*). To be concise, we draw on bi-directional inter-agency collaboration to countermove the, um, key takeaways underlying our annual dry-runs and aberrancy, (*clears throat*) that is *transparency* exercises as outlined in Recital number, huh, forgive me, I'll just have to whip through the latest amendments, and they are really voluminous, even for our standards (*throws a reproachful glance at REGULATOR*), of the, um, (*speaks even faster*) Double-D-GOOK Directive.

(*Coughs with a sudden sharp sound*) Alright.

(*Pours a glass of water, takes a sip, then speaks with fresh élan*)

I recall that today's meeting is part of an informal context-neutral negotiation protocol, reduced to its lowest level of granularity.

(*PARLIAMENTARIAN has an involuntary narcoleptic attack*)

The usual rules apply, as specified in the classified methodology booklet (*Holds up a thick manual*). No side-talks. No minutes. No note-taking. No private recordings (*Briefly looks up through thick glasses*). I need not remind you that the Tripartite format is a key element in improving the current way of working in our organisation, emphasising teamwork, overcoming silo mentalities, and harnessing synergies between portfolios.

(*Speaks perceptibly louder. PARLIAMENTARIAN wakes up*)

At today's authority table, we have three top-ranked representatives from, um (*REGULATOR and PARLIAMENTARIAN nod their heads in agreement*), well, the three pillars of our unified, um, insulated, body of (*REGULATOR and PARLIAMENTARIAN raise eyebrows*), um (*brief coughing*), I mean, um. I declare the session open.

(*Gulps down a large glass of water*)

On this afternoon's agenda, there's just one bullet point. (*Looks almost friendly*). So we should be done quickly.

(*Goes on talking so fast that it's nearly impossible to follow*)

Having regard to the functioning of the Treaty on the functioning of the Union, having regard to Regulation PU-666 on the interoperability of liquidity requirements, amending Regulation, um, on, um, and Decision number, um, and repealing Regulation, um, and in particular Article whatever, thereof, and (*with a voice of someone who has just inhaled of helium*), as per the reporting- and template-related instructions of the recently finalised, yet not ratified Excellence Policy Pact, wherein it is necessary to determine the competent authority for managing the remote control in the supra-prudential triumvirates, it should be decided as follows.

(*Articulates with care*) Any visual display of strategic information or otherwise must be handled by supervisors in an exclusive and orderly manner.

(*Takes a remote control out of her handbag and places it cautiously on the table. All eyes are on the little dark-grey object in front of her*)

(*Gets back to mechanical fast-talking*) A wide range of hybrid micro- and macro-policy instruments is now available at level two for designing a successful tier-one supra-national monitoring exchange architecture, varying from binge-, I mean, bench-marking to cross-referencing to hair-cutting to profit-shifting to stress-testing to goose-chasing over to quantitative teasing via pass-porting and, yes, let's face it, money slandering (*Throws a severe glance at her interlocutors*). Please be aware that there must be VERY deliberate consideration in terms of which tool should be used to switch on-and-off which player.

(*Looks up to the other protagonists, while her hand reaches out to the remote control*)

We refer to this technical aspect as the infrared-controlling-the-player problem. The ICPP, if you wish.

If you have further questions, you can seek input and assistance via a FAQ rubric on our secure intranet website. Passwords can be communicated in idiosyncratic situations only, as defined by the Charter of Fundamental Rights. A call-update-flash-info-answer has been added under the conditions-and-documents section. Well then, if there are no questions, we can close the meeting and rush over to our next.

(*Grabs the remote control, puts it back into her handbag, and starts to energetically stack together the piles of paper on her desk*)

Thank you for your attention.

(*Stands up. The other protagonists remain seated*)

PARLIAMENTARIAN: (*Loud voice, French accent*) *Madame* Chairman, if I may…

SUPERVISOR: I thank you for using gender-neutral language.

PARLIAMENTARIAN: Are you saying the supervisors will be in charge of operating the remote control of the beamer in the upcoming...?

SUPERVISOR: Please use core vocabulary only.

PARLIAMENTARIAN: (*Sighing. Speaking to himself*) Will we ever escape the doom-loop of technocracy?

SUPERVISOR: I urge you to focus on data.

PARLIAMENTARIAN: By what criteria do you justify this seizure of control? As far as I know, there is no evidence to legitimise...

SUPERVISOR: FYI, a criterion is a rule or principle that is used to judge, evaluate or test something. Evidence is the means by which a criterion may be proven. Ergo, concept of proof is not proof of concept.

PARLIAMENTARIAN: But this is just semantics, isn't it?

SUPERVISOR: I refer you to the updated Reference and Management of Nomenclatures manual in case you do not dispose of the vocabulary.

REGULATOR: (*Slight Italian accent*) All this fuss about a Powerpoint projection; what's more, in a closed-door meeting.

PARLIAMENTARIAN: Precisely. Let us not deny it, Mr Regulator, the power is the point.

REGULATOR: Well then, let's pretend to talk.

PARLIAMENTARIAN: It is my duty to protest against the autocratic *tournure* of this meeting. Do I have to remind you, *Madame*, that I am the citizens' voice? I'm democratically entrusted to…

SUPERVISOR: All right, then (*sits down again*), go on with your role-playing game, but please, play it by the playbook.

REGULATOR: Democracy is a nice word, honourable Member of Parliament. But you see, technically, the people you so forcefully represent are stupid. Most of them don't have a clue what's good for them.

PARLIAMENTARIAN: And you do?

(*REGULATOR laughs out loud*)

SUPERVISOR: In the absence of full-scale cross-cutting meta-data, such subjects are considered irrelevant.

PARLIAMENTARIAN: (*Ignores SUPERVISOR's remark*) There's a public sphere out there that wishes to make its voice heard. You mark my words, tomorrow at the latest I'm going to make a case in the hemicycle against the regulatory overkill that perverts the legal system.

REGULATOR: If the hemicycle isn't empty, as usual.

SUPERVISOR: I warn you, access to the content of off-the-record triangle meetings is restricted to a need-to-know basis, as disclosure might reasonably cause injury to the close-to-zero public interest, via an uncontrollable domino effect.

PARLIAMENTARIAN: *Madame Superviseur*, would you be so kind as to put that *télécommande* back to where it belongs (*knocks on the table*). Before it falls into the wrong hands.

REGULATOR: Any hands might be safer than those of brainless, far-left, far-right populists and such like, wouldn't you agree?

PARLIAMENTARIAN: (*Looks at SUPERVISOR, as if expecting her to take a position*) You two are conniving together!

REGULATOR: Surprised?

PARLIAMENTARIAN: I shall pen a rule-of-law report.

SUPERVISOR: Tick the appropriate box on the brown complaint form. In your folders.

REGULATOR: (*To PARLIAMENTARIAN*) Your lobby mates just LOVE the rule of law, don't they?

PARLIAMENTARIAN: I shall comply with your reporting rules, *Madame*. Nonetheless...

SUPERVISOR: Thank you. (*Takes the remote control out of her handbag and puts it back on the table, but possessively keeps her hand on it*). Without wanting to sound overconfident, I believe we have largely proved the sceptics wrong, and as such, I think we can close this fruitful discussion.

(*Clutches the device again*)

PARLIAMENTARIAN: (*Raises voice*) And leave YOU with the citizens' remote control?

SUPERVISOR: (*Calm tone*) The granularity adds waves to the edge…

(*As soon as the word 'granularity' is uttered, PARLIAMENTARIAN has another involuntary narcoleptic attack*)

REGULATOR: I'm tempted to look into the more esoteric parts of our, let's say, stimulatingly personal session of, how'd you call it, holistic surveillance brainstorming. (*Flirting*) Oh, Supervisor, if only I knew YOUR hypnotic power word…

SUPERVISOR: The underlying tone does not have to be nasty, colleague Regulator. The message must simply be very clear.

(*Puts remote control on the table at a safe distance from REGULATOR*)

REGULATOR: Meaning?

SUPERVISOR: The baseline assumes a gradual dissipation of global and domestic headwinds.

REGULATOR: No disorderly exit, then?

SUPERVISOR: The fiscal stance is expected to move from broadly neutral to tightening over the full horizon.

REGULATOR: Cash to grab? (*Brief smile*)

SUPERVISOR: That's the default option.

REGULATOR: What about the 2050 road-map?

SUPERVISOR: Risk-map.

REGULATOR: Whatever. Fading away of tailwinds, is that right?

SUPERVISOR: Taxpayers' problem, not ours.

REGULATOR: (*Mockingly*) Thus spoke the freshly appointed Head of the Single-Remote-Control-Radar. Praised be the Holy Trinity.

PARLIAMENTARIAN: (*Wakes up*) What am I doing here?

REGULATOR: Sleepwalking into oblivion.

PARLIAMENTARIAN: (*Loosens his tie*) It's unbearably hot and dry in here... I need fresh air.

REGULATOR: (*Jumps up, runs to the other side of the table, grabs the remote control*) Oh yeah, these overheated, windowless, depressurised, meeting-rooms (*laughing*), aren't they part of the Five Presidents' Cheap-Heat-Sleep- (*pushes the power button several time*) -Beep-Beep-Bubble-Complot?

SUPERVISOR: (*Furious*) The controller balances the subjects' rights to privacy with the public interest on a case-by-case basis.

REGULATOR: (*Equally irritated*) That's OUR job.

SUPERVISOR: Should I remind you that the cascade of rule-making goes on LONG after you REGs have completed your work?

REGULATOR: You are not the only sheriff in town, darling.

SUPERVISOR: It might not be possible to operate the remote control if the remote control eye is exposed to direct sunlight.

(*Walks around according to a chaotic pattern. Her stiletto shoes produce an annoying noise*)

REGULATOR: (*Following SUPERVISOR with his eyes*) Are we talking about a full-scale window of opportunity here?

(*SUPERVISOR briskly walks up to REGULATOR, looks him in the eyes. Stunned, he lowers his guard. She snatches the remote control and walks away. Turns to PARLIAMENTARIAN, who is still seated at the table, targets him with the device, pushes the power button. Then keeps walking around as noisily as before*)

PARLIAMENTARIAN: (*Speaks with SUPERVISOR's female voice and German accent*) Nuclear threats, zombie-firms and donut-bombs, trade-wars and ageing populations, fake news and global obesity, cyber-terrorism and chemical weather, illegal immigration and weapons of mass destruction...

(*Still with SUPERVISOR's voice, but strong French accent*)

Charity, austerity, prosperity, austerity, polarity, austerity, vulgarity, austerity, popularity, austerity...

SUPERVISOR: (*Presumptuous smile to REGULATOR*) A systemic hike is not entirely out of the ballpark.

PARLIAMENTARIAN: (*SUPERVISOR's shrill voice and German accent*) We resolutely data-drive through the next crisis-of-the-month.

REGULATOR: You lost me.

(*As SUPERVISOR passes by the table, she disdainfully throws on the ground the pile of papers she had previously arranged in an orderly stack*)

SUPERVISOR: Member states have not done their homework as they should!

REGULATOR: Bail them!

SUPERVISOR: Out or in?

REGULATOR: Funnily, those that are in want to be out, and those that are out want to be in again.

SUPERVISOR: We might soon be facing a cliff-edge threat.

REGULATOR: That a problem? We signed off on their living wills.

PARLIAMENTARIAN: (*With his normal voice*) Have we ended too big to fail? Or have we simply failed too big?

(*SUPERVISOR desperately triggers the remote control in his direction, but to no effect*)

REGULATOR: (*Laughs*) Out of control?

SUPERVISOR: (*Goes up to REGULATOR and shouts viciously*) Mr Granulator!

PARLIAMENTARIAN: (*Screams, while fighting against irresistible desire to sleep*) Don't you dare!

REGULATOR: Don't worry, we only simulated failure.

PARLIAMENTARIAN: (*Weak voice*) Stimulated, you mean! (*Falls asleep straightaway*)

REGULATOR: (*To SUPERVISOR*) Did we manage to keep the framework simple?

SUPERVISOR: I believe we did a good job.

(*Throws remote control in her bag*)

In a nutshell.

The Illusion of Europe

Caroline Muscat

IT TOOK A MURDER to make me realise that the Europe we thought we were living in isn't the Europe we're inhabiting.

The victim was my friend, Daphne Caruana Galizia. She was a journalist writing about corruption at the centre of government in Malta, the EU's smallest member state. Her brutal assassination by car bomb – in broad daylight, just down the road from her home – shocked us all and exposed an ugliness I thought we'd outgrown.

Daphne established herself early in her career as a fiery political commentator. She believed in European liberal values and fought for a free and open society, one that would promote an integrity and accountability so lacking in the country's political class.

She took on criminal gangs, corrupt politicians and shady governments, driven by her uncompromising sense of right and wrong.

But she was so much more than just a journalist whose articles often set the country's political agenda. She was a daughter, a sister, a wife and mother of three highly accomplished sons. She loved tending her garden. She went back to university to study Archaeology. And she published a magazine called *Taste & Flair,* dedicated to beautiful things: the polar opposite of the world she wrote about on her *Running Commentary* blog or in her column.

I'd often met her in passing, but I first got to know Daphne when I published the results of my investigation into a property scandal that revealed collusion between the Government of Malta and a local businessman. Daphne was the first to call me and offer support. She warned me of the torrent of abuse I would receive as a result of my story, and she shared further details on the background and context.

We became friends when I fell ill the following year. She checked in on me regularly when I was homebound, and when my doctor called to tell me the worst was over, Daphne was there to hold me as my legs gave out. She understood just how much I'd gone through without either of us saying a word. It was in that moment of silent contact that I understood how deeply she cared. The boldness in her writing stemmed from a passion for the principles she upheld so strongly.

Daphne wanted a better Malta, one built on European values. She fought so ferociously because she couldn't stand injustice. She was hated for holding up a mirror to people's worst version of themselves, but she was loved in equal measure by those she inspired.

Anyone who wanted to know what was happening in the country went to Daphne's blog first. Her writing was forceful, blunt and personal, and her style was undiluted. *Politico* called her 'a one-woman WikiLeaks.' She was impossible to ignore.

She was also impossible to intimidate – and so many in Malta tried. Her front door was set on fire. Her family dog's throat was slit, its body laid across her doorstep. Petrol-filled tires were stacked against the rear wall of her home and set ablaze as the family slept. Politicians and businessmen hounded her with libel suits.

Still, she refused to back down. Her only vulnerability was that she was out on a limb. The attacks against her started when Malta was not part of the EU, but the country's membership did not put an end to them. They intensified until she was killed.

The last words Daphne wrote on her blog have been quoted around the world. 'There are crooks everywhere you look now. The situation is desperate.'

Minutes after publishing it, she drove away from her house, where a man watching from a hill sent a message to another man stationed in a boat out at sea. Police investigations revealed that a bomb had been placed beneath the seat of her car, and they triggered it.

A neighbour who saw Daphne driving down the hill reported two explosions, not one. The first tore her leg off. But she'd only just begun to scream when, seconds later, a larger explosion engulfed her car in a ball of fire.

How could this happen in Europe, a region once considered a sanctuary for journalists? A few months later, investigative journalist Ján Kuciak and his fiancée Martina Kušnírová were shot dead in their home in Slovakia.

Are we to accept the murder of journalists as a new norm?

These are brutal messages intended to silence us all. We have an obligation to fight back. These acts didn't just target Daphne and Ján and Martina. They were aimed at freedom of expression and citizens' right to know. But nobody, not even those in power, can take them away from us with impunity.

Most of us were deeply shocked by Daphne's death, but as her assassination made international headlines, members of pro-government Facebook groups met the news with calls for 'celebration'.

An investigation by *The Shift News* infiltrated these restricted groups, where we found comments that described

Daphne as a '*saḥḥara ḥadra*' (an evil witch) and called for her to burn in hell.

Other commenters posted things like, 'she got what she deserved', 'what goes around comes around', and 'she can't rest in peace because she's in pieces, she can't even be buried, karma is a bitch.'

The President, Prime Minister Joseph Muscat, and eight of his senior staff were members of these groups, where Muscat was worshipped as 'il-King ta' Malta' (the King of Malta), and where the personal details of anti-corruption activists were distributed, along with calls for them to be physically attacked, sexually assaulted and stalked.

Malta is a deeply misogynistic society. It's always been that way. Daphne wasn't just attacked for her writing, she was targeted for who she was: a woman working in a country where a woman speaking her mind is seen as 'aggressive', 'hysterical', 'abrasive' and 'hormonal'.

The 'Mediterranean Man' provided fuel for some of our lunchtime conversations. The image of the tanned hunk, bare-chested with six-pack abs, was largely the stuff of fiction. Most Maltese men we knew were lumpy, overweight mammy's boys who expected to go from a pampered life with their devoted ma to being spoiled by a wife, without having to do anything in between.

It remains difficult for a woman to get ahead, even when she's so much more competent than her counterparts. Women who are bold and at the forefront of their journalistic professions have to deal with threats and language men don't face.

The EU held such hope for Malta. We didn't trust our own politicians to get things right, and so we voted to join, thinking our membership would prevent a recurrence of past governmental abuses.

And there was hope, at least for a while. But we took so much for granted. One of them was the belief that Europe would save us from our own worst impulses.

The rot within the Maltese system floated to the surface in 2013, when the people elected Joseph Muscat's Labour government. Muscat had been one of the EU's main opponents. Overnight, institutions that should be serving the public interest began to serve those who could pull their strings. And I mean 'overnight' quite literally. Daphne was the first to reveal that the Panama Papers would expose the fact that top ministers within Labour set up shell companies in Panama within days of winning the election.

With alarming speed, we watched the collapse of the rule of law under Muscat's leadership, and with it, a disintegration of the European values our country was meant to uphold. For impunity to reign so blatantly, the system had to be poisoned at the roots.

But how easily our system – and those of other member states – catered to it. We voted in populists who exploited citizens' scepticism of vulnerable institutions, and those citizens accepted it as another part of the new normal.

Technology fed into this populism as digital platforms – which held so much democratic promise for opening up access to information and debate across communities and countries – ended up being used as tools of repression. The pro-government trolls who hounded Daphne and celebrated her death in groups linked to the Party in power were just symptoms of the larger threat social media has come to pose.

The nature of social media siloing has meant that we're now focussed almost exclusively on what divides us as individuals, nation states and tribes, rather than on what holds us together as Europeans. The Cambridge Analytica scandal also revealed how easily these platforms could be used to manipulate public opinion for private gain.

Our institutions need the capability to deal with these rapid technological changes, and they also need robust mechanisms to compel member states to uphold our shared values. Right now, we're lacking both.

So what's the solution?

The European Union survived because of its approach to openness and accessibility. It isn't perfect by any stretch, but it's better than the wars that preceded it. It can be fixed. The 'how' is up to all of us; but we can start by defending what worked.

As a journalist, I believe freedom of expression, freedom of opinion, and the right to information have provided the essential foundation for our shared European values. When these freedoms erode, the entire structure crumbles.

We need the freedom to hold power to account. That has long been the role of the press. But it is also the freedom – the obligation – to bring our disagreements into the open. To discuss our concerns and our fears, to argue passionately over them, and by doing so, to come to a consensus that we can all support. Avoiding uncomfortable discussions only pushes them below the surface, where they fester into ugly nationalisms or intolerant populist leaders.

Europe has traditionally defended these freedoms, even going so far as to advocate for the safety of journalists in totalitarian countries and failed states. But for the first time since the end of the Cold War, these freedoms are under threat here at home.

Daphne's violent death forced Europe to pay attention to Malta. As the murder investigation dragged on, it became obvious to outside observers that we were no closer to learning who ordered her assassination. Despite calls for an independent public inquiry, the Government of Malta has done everything it can to avoid that outcome.

A number of international institutions have sent delegations to our island, including the Council of Europe and the European Parliament. Each went home more alarmed than they were when they arrived.

At least they've finally begun to understand that this is not just a Malta problem. This is about the rule of law and democracy in Europe. Our island is just one theatre in a much larger conflict.

The Europe I believed in looked nothing like these crippled institutions struggling to create pressure for justice for Daphne's murder. But this is the Europe we live in right now.

The last thing Daphne said to me, a few days before her assassination, was, 'I get a sense of time running out. There are so many things I wanted to do that I haven't done.'

The values she died fighting for are the values that united us. It's time we start living up to them with our actions, not just our words.

Another Rosy-fingered Dawn for Europe?

Gloria Wekker

ONE EVENING IN THE dead of winter 2015, close to zero degrees and with a cold wind searching out everyone's bones, my longtime friend Marjan showed up at our door in Amsterdam with two men who turned out to be refugees from Somalia and Eritrea: Mo and Abdou. Marjan had been active with the undocumented refugee group 'We Are Here' since 2012, helping the men and women move from one relinquished apartment building to another empty church in Amsterdam; they had been squatting for years, being chased like vermin by the police. Now the group had recently relocated to a vacant garage in our neighbourhood, a huge empty shell without any facilities, like water or electricity. The garage was a desolate and dangerous place of last resort. Marjan had talked to me about the various needs of the group: money needed to be donated for food, for transport, for visits to the doctor, to court or to the IND, the Immigration and Naturalisation Service, the institution responsible for deciding on refugees' applications for permits to stay. But there were also daily needs to be met, like having their clothes washed, warm blankets and clothing, being able to take a shower. I had, thus far, contented myself with donating money and had not expected her to show up at my door. Meeting Mo and Abdou was raw and chilling, very uncomfortable to be face to face with real people, '*no future*' written all over them, while they must have been in their thirties, the face of Europe's latest wave of hysteria. The men were hungry, cold and in bad need of a shower. My lover Maggy and I fed them, drank red wine with them, talked about the families they had left behind. When they left past midnight, we felt an awkward mixture of being wholly inadequate, powerless, full of shame at our warm house, and food that we could easily share. We were acutely aware of the sheer luck, in my case, of having been born with a European passport or, in Maggy's, having been able to obtain it relatively easily. Even though we had, in the eyes of a growing group of people in Dutch society, the wrong bodies for the passport, as both of us had been born in Suriname – a part of the Dutch Kingdom until 1975 – our fates had been sealed in a fortunate way. Their misfortune, their crime was to have been born in the wrong countries, with the wrong passports, being dispensable and unwanted, card-carrying members of the tribe that Europe has declared unfit to enter and to live among us. Their most likely future in Europe was and is death. There but for the grace of the goddess…!

Europe has meant many different things throughout history. 'Rosy-fingered,' Greek poet Homer called the dawn of Europe, containing a promise of beautiful things to come. In some respects, Homer was right: in terms of music, painting, writing, Europe has been rosy-fingered, it has delivered on the promise. In others, notably humanitarianism, it has failed miserably. During the colonial period, white people in the Dutch colonies of the East Indies and Suriname identified with and called themselves 'Europeans', not Norwegians, Dutch or British. An imaginary unity was bred, far away from home, while in the heartland of Europe itself, national identifications remained paramount. Fast forward several centuries and we see a new incarnation of Europe: for some, a necessary focal point, the only chance at global economic, political and cultural survival; while for others Europe has come to represent an undesirable configuration, one that takes away power and cherished identity from national entities, endangering their autonomy. Brexit and other attempts at leaving or merely taking advantage of the benefits of the European Union illustrate this ongoing tense relationship to a transnational Europe, which is accompanied by unprecedented waves of nationalism, xenophobia and resentment. The death of many African, Middle Eastern and Asian refugees at the borders of Europe is a price we are momentarily shocked by, but willing to pay, if we can continue to turn a blind eye to and be spared the sight of refugees at our doorstep. Immoral deals with Turkey and with Libya to stop the refugees before they reach Europe, the cooping up of tens of thousands of refugees in Greece and Italy, like they were chickens, reneging, except for Malta and Finland, on our EU-wide promises, are defended by even the left. The majority of European citizens is lulled into thinking that we are doing our utmost in an impossible situation that we have not asked for, that 'we have nothing to do with'. Is this the best that we can do? Seriously?

I am struck by the bitter continuities and the utter lack of shame manifesting in European political attitudes towards the non-European Other during the colonial era and now. Entitlement impelled many European nations to travel halfway across the world, in order to take possession of different territories, sometimes importing new populations but always subjugating them, appropriating their resources and making enormous profits. While there was no question of egalitarianism between white European colonisers and the colonised, sexual relations of male colonisers with colonised women were, of course, exempted from the general rule of 'not going native' and resulted in mixed populations almost everywhere. Importantly, such relations also inexorably pointed to deep patterns of Western hypocrisy, which have not gone unnoticed by the colonised. In the wake of these 'adventurous', proud accomplishments, deep and abiding chasms were installed between North and South in access to valuable knowledge and resources, which were often appropriated from the local populations; unequal access to capital, to ways of making a living, to prosperity. In addition, a cultural archive was established that provided Europeans with a unique sense of superiority, accomplishment, excellence and a deep sense of the inevitability of the course that history took. Europe's was a sacred mission to bring civilisation to these downtrodden, uncivilised folks and that particular effect, cemented in its cultural archive, is still operative now towards people of colour. On the basis of these divergent roots and routes of development, the tables have been turned in terms of who is doing the travelling now: 'We have come here because you were there.' That reverse travelling and especially the arrival has become increasingly difficult in all kinds of respects.

In the summer of 2010, Maggy and I travelled to the Dominican Republic for my work, trying to establish collaboration with colleagues in Gender Studies there. Eventually, the mission was not successful, due to language difficulties, but apart from that, European passports in hand, we had no problems whatsoever. It was an extraordinary experience to encounter a Caribbean society, inflected by Spanish architecture and culture. We met and befriended a woman, let's call her Dora, who worked in the hotel where we stayed and a couple of months later, she came to visit us in Amsterdam, at our invitation. Her arrival at Schiphol airport was sheer drama: waiting for hours, after the plane had landed, she still had not shown up, until my name was announced on the intercom. I had to come to the office of the Military Police at the airport, in order to verify who I was and whether I had the financial means to support Dora during her stay. It was not sufficient that I verbally stated that I was able to do so, I had to digitally show them the amount of money in my bank and savings accounts and what my monthly income was. My distinct impression was that she, hailing from the Dominican Republic, was seen as a sex worker, having come to The Netherlands to make money and that I, as a black woman, did not exactly fulfil the visible requirements of a credible host. In a world that has become increasingly globalised, particular representations of men and women of colour, have become stuck. One of my PhD students from Taiwan was, upon her first arrival, interrogated at Schiphol and asked, even though they knew her professional status, whether the real reason for her coming to The Netherlands, was finding a Dutch man. Her white Canadian colleague who arrived the same day was spared such intrusive questioning. Racialising moves that have been installed in our cultural archive have not lost their purchase. No matter how removed Dora, in reality, was from the branch of work that the police imputed to her, this stamp was automatically put on her. I was not only mortified and hurt by her treatment at the airport on her first visit, also her very first international travel, I was also painfully aware of the fact that I, as a full university professor, but first and foremost guilty of being a black woman, had to show my bank statements. Sexism, racism and classism were on full display in both our cases. It was one of those familiar moments when even having the right passport is not enough, the carrier of colour also needs to show her credentials, i.e. she does not automatically share in the privileges accorded to white citizens, to be bona fide.

In between being aware of the privileges of having a Dutch passport, yet being livid and ashamed at the treatment people of colour, myself included, receive at the hands of Dutch (border) police, what can we, people who have some measure of historical knowledge and ethical and political responsibility, do in order to make another moment of rosy-fingeredness in Europe, possible? Let us first be reminded of Toni Morrison's words in her beautiful essay 'Home' (1998):

> *I have never lived, nor have any of us, in a world in which race did not matter. Such a world, free of racial hierarchy, is usually imagined or described as dreamscape, Edenesque, utopian, so remote are the possibilities of its achievement…* <u>*How to be both free and situated: how to convert a racist house into a race-specific yet non-racist home. How to enunciate race while depriving it of its lethal cling?*</u>

Underlined in this quote is the programme we need to work towards to attain another rosy-fingered Europe. In the first place, we need to become aware of and dismantle the cultural archive that was installed and cemented in European populations, in the framework of imperialism, since the sixteenth century. A racial grammar, a deep structure of inequality in thought and affect based on race, was installed in European populations, whether they actually did have an Empire or not, and it is from this deep reservoir, this cultural archive, that, a sense of a superior, innocent self was formed. This self-representation tells us Europeans that since we are, by our own acclamation, non-racist, nothing that we do or say, can be racist. We need to fundamentally rid ourselves of the self-flattering understanding that 'racism is done elsewhere, in the USA, in South Africa, but not here. *We* do not do race'.

Secondly, we need to ask why there is no serious investigation into the possibilities of having people from the

South enter and work in Europe under regular conditions. This would entail getting rid of deplorable treaties like the Dublin Claim, incarcerating people in their first country of arrival. Why do we spend our appreciable financial resources in keeping them out or cooping them up, instead of making a decent way of life in Europe possible for them, in which periodic return migration becomes feasible? Why do we want the benefits of globalisation only for ourselves, not for Others?

The issue, finally, is whether we allow our basest fears and anxieties to define who we are as Europeans, continuing to deny the historical advantages taken by this continent at the expense of others.

With thanks to Marjan Sax

The Void

Bronka Nowicka

Introduction

URIAH: Where are their mouths?

TOBIAS: On their faces.

URIAH: Ours are in our hearts.

SEMEL: That's what separates the craftsmen from people.

TOBIAS: Do they think they make themselves?

SEMEL: They believe they happen unto themselves.

TOBIAS: Have they stopped practising the firmament?

SEMEL: They don't even oil the machines that join things.

URIAH: Are they able to be a flock of birds and scatter?

SEMEL: They have closed the lending libraries of animal bodies. Now they mock those bodies before the slaughter.

URIAH: Do they ask how landscapes see them?

SEMEL: They forgot what it is to cast a soul onto a landscape.

TOBIAS: Can they recall the art of turning the elements around?

SEMEL: They've never heard of flying fish or burrowing birds.

URIAH: What about the roads they haven't taken? Do they still venerate them?

SEMEL: They fashion small boxes to hold annihilation.

TOBIAS: How do they yearn?

SEMEL: They need not raze their cities to forget someone.

TOBIAS: What about love?

SEMEL: They rear herds of desires. Their bodies calve.

TOBIAS: Do they take lessons on loss?

SEMEL: No longer.

URIAH: Do they have dreams?

SEMEL: Hobbled ones.

URIAH: Do they try and learn from those dreams who the answer might be?

SEMEL: They don't even know who the question is.

Arrival

By that time, we were only making fragments, for we had grown incapable of comprehending wholes. The history of the world had got too long for us, much like our own histories. We were taking shorter roads to learning, not much more than arm's lengths. Our arms we used for parcels. Our legs we used little. We were not running forth into the future, nor were we returning to the past. Every day we would begin anew and mumble our way through our existential refrains. The day we were called, we boarded the train without question, though we knew the destination not. For many days the landscapes ran alongside our compartments, only to always lose the race and wind up behind us. Then came the Void.

When everything vanished, we sought succour in language. We tried to name the things we didn't know in an effort to disentangle ourselves from that vacuum – putting up sentences like roofs over our heads. But our mouths housed only restless worms now. They would try to crawl down towards our chins before realising they were attached at our throats. Then they would retreat to their burrows, only to wander back out and onto our faces soon after. They refused to extract the material we required to describe. And so we stood mute in something similar in colour to winter. It certainly had the appearance of a season. The wind had not died down and was blowing from the north, so we went in that direction.

We wandered through the milk dissolved in time until we were standing at the seaside. Its hefty body lay there, fully occupied with respiration. It meditated, recollecting comets. Our presence had no significance to it. Nearby, three men frolicked in a wave that was unaware of their games. They ran after it whenever it retreated. When it would return and be about to catch up with them, they would slip away. They were like children playing with a sleeping mother's hair, taking mischievous advantage of her steady slumber. Noticing us, they grew serious. They proclaimed that they were master craftsmen, from whom we were to learn.

Workshop

And we had been rocked,
once the bells were hung inside us

Speech Lesson

Since the appearance of the Void, we have not eaten. The stronger among us are still sitting upright, but most have lain down in the sand. The waves rise and wrap around the waists of those lying in the sand. The water undresses us and takes away our shoes. In silence, we acquiesce to that most innocent of thefts an element may come to. Motionless on the shore, we look like a sick herd. We ask the craftsmen for something to eat, but they provide us with nothing. They insist only a famished person will be able to master speech.

'Whisper bread balls,' they instruct us.

We don't understand, so we set about to die. Slowly fading, we pronounce the names of human beings and animals, wishing to fete existence in some audible form. We repeat the words for old truths and events. We turn our heads to those lying beside us and pass our utterances from mouth to mouth. They fortify like wine apples, like honey, like sugar cubes.

Looking Lesson

They bring in an old man. They ask us to look.

Seated, he moves his jaw like scissors. He cuts up a vision of the world into intelligible pieces. Once he must have sliced bread in this same way. Suddenly a tic breaks out over the old man's face – and it shatters his defenceless expression. Afraid, he sends his hands up to tidy the rubble. They work in the sweat of his forehead until the next face mine goes off. He bends, holds his knees in his hands – not wanting to lose his slim bundle of tinder. He stands; he toddles to the left, veers right. He is lost and asks:

'Which way to myself?'

'You aren't looking,' the craftsmen say. 'You're merely viewing. If that is what you're using your eyes for, you're better off just keeping them shut.'

Then we look in the way they have taught us. Before our gazes reach the old man, we wrap them in rags and dampen them in warm water. They glide over his temples, nape, throat. We rinse him so he falls asleep. Then we, too, are permitted to let down our eyelids.

Yearning Lesson

We dig a hole. When it is deep enough, they lay a wooden beam before it, Thus they set the threshold that divides the kingdoms. And we are not permitted to cross this threshold, even leaning in over the crater, crying out for our mothers.

'If they're in the ground, they will come out,' the master craftsmen say.

No one comes, so we sit on the beach and are flooded with dreams.

At dawn the mothers wake us for a clapping game: they run in a ring, catching the wind in their shirts. They raise their skirts up over their stick-legs. They stretch out their arms, turning into sails. They laugh, letting their braids come undone. Turning, they feel like figures on a vast carousel over a broken mechanism, now in motion.

'Come here,' they call. They want to take us for a spin.

We rise and take steps as wobbly as our first. The mothers bend down, reach out as they once did, back when they were there to catch us.

When we try to cross the threshold, they disappear. Then they're gone again, and we find our thumbs in our mouths. We catch our own bodies swaying.

Remembering Lesson

'I'm just a boy back then,' one of us recalls. 'My father is taking me into the forest at night. There the darkness strips us of our shapes and hangs them up in the trees like coats. From then on – two naked voices – we walk without bodies. As we get further away, animals go up to them. They lick their hands, butt their heads into the legs we left behind. I am scared we will not find the road back to ourselves. We will not find ourselves, because the foxes will borrow us and run off in us. The paternal voice comes soothing. It gets so low I can hear it right by the ground. It envelops me, gets covered in fur I can hold onto.'

'You have received memory,' says a craftsman. 'You do not know the art of erasure. The techniques of forgetting are foreign to you. It will sometimes happen that a man and a child will pass through you. Make them a soft road to tread. Turn off the lights. Let your insides get covered in moss.'

Forgiveness Lesson

The craftsmen call out over the hole.

The mother of one of us stands on the threshold, and in her hand, which is trembling, she holds the news. She beckons to her son with her palm upright and cupped, like a boat, as though it held upon it some newly hatched occurrence.

'Once, when you weren't there, there was a cricket drowning in one of our old pots. I took him out, but he wasn't moving. I thought: *It'll surely go to waste, but I'll give him a leaf.* I went and did something and then went to check on him. There he was, sitting, eating his meal.'

Here the mother pauses to nod.

'Just miraculous, the mechanisms behind each little thing,' she says. 'He had such tiny little jaws. They moved as he chewed.'

We picture her bent over that spared cricket, trying to glean the meaning of the universe from the architecture of an insect's face. Then we forgive her – for everything. One of us for the fact that she gave sad milk.

Feeding Lesson

'A long time ago, feeding had very little to do with the mouth,' explains Tobias. 'Maybe only insofar as it opened a little while edible images were being admired. Most people back then fed with their eyes.'

Women handled the cooking. During the day, they would go out for clay so they could burn the sienna, umber, ochre. They'd drag basketfuls of coal and chalk into the kitchen. They'd grind bones and shells into powder in their querns. In the forest, they would look for horsehair, pick up pine needles. They kept resin in vessels – little lumps of dammar gum, sandarac. At night they would plan their canvases:

• a bit of linen • a fish • rainwater • a fistful of white stones • sap • ash • a buttress root • snow • salt

First, clarify the rainwater, and soak the fabric. Then, wipe off the stones, and combine them with the sap. Dip the fish in this before coating it in ash. Wring out the linen and spread it over the ground, rubbing in the salt. Lay the root down along the edges of the canvas – make a frame. Put the fish in the middle. In winter, sprinkle in snow pellets or grated black ice. In summer, use soot. Keep the food black and white. When everyone has looked their fill, roll the image up.

The blind and the visually impaired would eat with their skin. Persons less sensitive to touch could open sounds – just as later people might halve mussels or nuts – and use their fingers to dig out these sounds' contents. In the age of eating with the senses, no one went hungry.

Enjoyment Lesson

It's hot. We drag along the embankment like oxen harnessed to our own shadows. We are looking for a place for a bell – so the craftsmen have instructed us.

We're on the lookout for a cathedral, even if it's only a mirage. We dream up towers. Then, as we race around with ever-growing panic, we dream up a mere hook on a beam, a common loop of rope. But there is nothing other than land or water. Hours go by – we are hourglasses, going back and forth across the sand. We find nothing.

'The bell's outlet,' say the craftsmen, 'is known as its "mouth". It is bounded by lips, and the sound it makes is talking. Inside is its heart. Its sides are mantle. Above it: the neck; further up is its crown. It is an instrument created in your likeness.'

Listening to them, some show their palates, others the concave place between their ribs. For a moment, we feel the weight of the craftsmen hanging bronze inside us. Later, ringing, we run in the direction of the water that will carry our toll.

Creating Lesson

bird

'When forming a bird, remember it's little more than covering over a voice,' says Uriah. 'Take the sound and wrap it in flesh. Cover the flesh in down. Dandelion would be good, or poplar tufts, white fluffy snow is not as good – you'll get it off a short-lived animal. For the beak use horn. Shape the makeshift bones out of matches. Make sure to sew up the twin sacs for the lungs. Inflate them and put them inside. Finally, apply the colour, although you do not have to. Song will carry even in a thing as grey as packing paper.

dog

'A dog will not complain of its material. You can put it together from whatever you have to hand. Even the scrappiest will evince loyalty and a will to live. Slipshod mutts, coming apart at the seams or half squashed will all be faithful. Those whose eyes have not yet been put in, whose paws remain uncarved, will jump to life before the job can even be finished. They rejoice, they leap, pure hobbling perfection. They run in order to collide. Rolling around in the straw, they spark. Stuffed with inferior materials, they burn, and in a flash, are gone. And so the untrained craftsman must never take a dog into the workshop,' Semel concludes.

Departure

Our own hands woke us. They took our lain-down heads and turned them to the light like bristle-covered stones. They carved faces into them, and when they had finished, they opened our eyes and stayed there, suspended in front of them. Turning over, our hands demonstrated who they really were: living tools ready to smite inaction. We rose, hastened by snapped fingers.

The craftsmen were nowhere. They weren't sitting, as they had in the past, on a dune; nor were they frolicking in the sea. We cried out, but no one shouted back. They had gone. On the shore stood a wooden shed. When we opened the door, we saw a table, and beside it a heap of clay. At the bases of the walls lay tree trunks, coils of wire, sheets of metal and crushed glass. There were jars of paint. Mangers held balls of wool, others paper, feathers, myrrh.

Our hands drew us into the shed. There they rolled up their sleeves and started crafting in the Void. They set about creating the world.

Translated from the Polish by Jennifer Croft

The Voice Inside my Head

Ana Pessoa

AND THAT'S WHY I LOVE the night, this dark silence, when all I can hear is my breathing, my breathing in the world, my breathing inside and outside my body and nothing else, no colour, no sun, no sounds, a dark loneliness inside and outside the room, a pause in life, and all of a sudden I know something about myself, something I didn't know before or didn't know I knew, me, the sixteen-year-old boy, me, the boy from the 22nd century, my body so still and quiet in the still and quiet night, the dark and empty and vast and lovely night, my eyes closed and my soul open to the stars that sit so far away in the sky and look so small and weak, but are in fact big and strong, and I think about the voice inside my head, this voice inside my head, this voice that belongs to me but is not mine, the technological voice that speaks and affirms and insists, and I know it has no impact on the universe, this voice is so much bigger than me and yet it doesn't even exist in space, it emits no light, it generates nothing, it doesn't move, and the noise can't be heard in the night, it can't be heard from the stars, and I think about this immense mystery that will continue to be an immense mystery after I'm gone, with its galaxies and black holes, I think about the questions that will still be questions, and I feel a sense of relief, a new sense of comfort inside and outside myself, comfort in my head and on my pillow, because I am nothing, I'm absolutely nothing, I'm sixteen years old and I have a voice inside my head, I'm still and quiet in the still and quiet night with my loneliness and my silence, lying on the bed, a kind of death that is nothing like death, that is really the opposite of death, because I am alive, I am completely alive inside and outside myself, I'm completely alive in the darkness and the empty space, and I hear nothing other than my own breathing, the air coming in and out, life coming in and out, night coming in and out, and I don't have that voice inside my head telling me that everything has a solution, that my feelings are identical to other people's feelings, that my loneliness is identical to other people's loneliness, and I don't want to know about other people's loneliness, I ask myself where I end and where this programmed voice begins, where I end and where technology begins, where technology begins and where I end, because I am not this voice inside my head, I don't want to hear the voice inside my head, I want to be alone, in silence, in the dark, because only the night understands me, only the night will save me, the night with its full, real darkness is the only thing that truly illuminates, and I lie and think about this pitch black, frigid night, and the bats that inhabit this pitch black, frigid night, and their caves, their inverted slumber, upside down and diurnal, and I think that I should be a solitary bat with huge wings, I should be a nocturnal animal, a rat, a cat, a coyote, a hyena, I've always thought I was born into the wrong body, the wrong species, the wrong era, a leopard, a cockroach, a scorpion, I should be a yellow-eyed owl soaring inaudibly over the world with a curved, short, sharp beak, a carnivorous, predatory, watchful nature, an easy wisdom that comes from silence and stealth, a nocturnal power that might counter the voice inside my head, the perpetual voice, interrupting all my thoughts, telling me to 'do this', 'do that', 'go here', 'go there', this technological voice that accompanies me down every street and in every moment, telling me that my impatience is a clear sign of stress, that I'm not considering the consequences of my decisions, that I'm not alone, that I'm never alone, and there is no greater loneliness than this, the loneliness of company, inner loneliness, hidden, clandestine, nocturnal loneliness, the feeling that there should be more to life than this, the streets, the metro stations, the restaurants, the conversations, the people and the paving stones, the classrooms, the waiting rooms; the hope that there's life beyond life, not life beyond death, because death is like darkness, unmistakeable and all-encompassing; and that's when I hear the voice inside my head, always the voice inside my head, recommending sleep and dreams, suggesting what time I get up at, telling me to avoid salt and sugar and to take iron and magnesium supplements, the voice asking me questions, (why, where, how, when), talking to me about another era, for example, about the end of Europe, the end of democracy, telling me that my life today is better than any other life in the past, explaining all the things I don't want to be explained, and even now, as the night arrives with its rough, dark body, even in this existence without colour and sun and sound, the voice exists and I hear it, I can make it out in the darkness, a hushed voice saying 'I'm here', the made-up voice that doesn't even belong to me, which never did and never will because it's not human, the artificial, technological voice that disseminates itself, scatters, talks to me like a person, like another mother, so different from my real mother, who also hears this voice inside her head, the imaginary voice, the voice of the system inside every head, and I ask myself where technology begins and the human body ends, if technology runs inside my body like my blood and my soul and my dreams and my fears, and I just want to run, run, run, fast and silent and huge like a leopard in the depths of night, with my hunger, running in this black, frigid night, with my four swift paws, and my body that is no longer my body, was never my body, and I so badly want the old one back, my body before the voice and the pain, my body and the night, my body and the silence, and maybe I'd be happier in the past, in the 20th century, the 21st century, in that Europe of lonely people who, in spite of everything, were free and thought and felt without the noise, without interferences, without the technology inside their heads, their minds calm and quiet, and then the voice interrupts my thoughts and tells me that loneliness was the biggest epidemic of the 21st century, that the voice inside my head came along to deal with loneliness and that I'm talking like a poet, that I should write like a poet, but I don't talk like a poet and I don't write like a poet, because I don't know how to feel or think or exist, I just want to be in silence, and I'm so sick of being told what I should or shouldn't do, I'm really sick of that faceless disembodied voice, the strange feeling that my life is not really my life, that I am not myself, that I don't make my own decisions because everything was set out for me and on my behalf, and the voice laughs, a dark, concealed laugh that's not quite a laugh, like the way hyenas laugh, laughing but not really laughing, the voice inside my head interrupting and interfering and interrogating, telling me I am the master of my own will, that I am the one who makes the decisions, and it's not true, I know it's not true and the voice of the system also knows, because this voice inside my head knows everything about everything, the voice inside my head that tells me what is true, and it's so certain of itself and so full of answers, and I'm so full of questions, and that's when I realise how tired I am, when I feel the weight of my inexistence in my legs and I just want to sleep, I just want to go back to dreaming about whales, dark and enormous like the depths of night, I'm hollow and submissive like an empty waiting room, a row of chairs with no one sitting on them, and I look at the waiting room that is myself and I feel sad, wretched, useless, the voice always here, telling me that sadness is normal, that sadness is just that, a passing sadness, the voice asking me 'How would you rate your sadness on a scale of 1 to 10,' and I don't want to rate sadness, I don't want to quantify sadness, I want to feel and to suffer because my sadness is real, my sadness is a fact, my sadness is my truth, my voice, my existence, and I force myself not to listen to the voice inside my head, telling me I'll get to my destination quicker if I take the metro, when I don't even have a destination, when I have nothing apart from this pitch black night and my sad, sad sadness, and the voice tells me that maybe I should talk about all this to Su, because Su is my friend and she likes me and I like her, the voice inside my head is telling me that my sadness might go away when I'm with Su, and I think of Su with this voice inside her head and I imagine another Su, Su from the past, before all this, Su before the voice, the fully human Su, with no voice, with no technology, Su and I in another age, in the 21st century, in that world without voices inside your head, Su is as real and vast and beautiful as this pitch black night, and then I see a sky inside me, I see my sadness flying off into the horizon, a solitary owl flying silently off into space, and the voice interrupts my dream to tell me about Su, to ask me about Su and I don't want to talk about Su, I don't want to understand Su or explain Su or discuss Su, especially not Su, and I don't want any more of the voice inside my head's suggestions or opinions or predictions, I just want to be by myself, to think by myself, to feel by myself, I want to be free and find my truth like the coyote and the bat living their nocturnal lives, so I let out a silent scream and lie there listening to that imaginary scream that belongs to me, my voice stretching out in time and space, my scream that exists in this world and in all the other worlds, my scream that is enormous and infinite like the universe, and no one can stop this scream, which doesn't exist either, because in reality I am still and quiet in the still, quiet night, my eyes closed and my soul open, the silence resting upon everything, my lonely, lonely loneliness, and yes, now I really can be who I want, I can fall asleep in this bed and dream about whales, as gigantic and dark and slow as the night, now and forever, and I can be an owl and I can leave through the window, silent and watchful, and I can talk like a poet and write like a poet and scream like a poet, because I come from space and from the infinite, my imaginary scream out into the silence of the stars which dwell so far away and look so small and weak but are in fact big and strong, and I'm nothing, I'm absolutely nothing and nor is the voice inside my head, this great voice, so much bigger than I am that it doesn't even belong to the universe, so I open my eyes and get up, I feel my feet and hands, my body existing in this world and in all the other worlds, and for a dark moment, one which stretches out into space like an entire landscape, I know exactly who I am.

Translated from the Portuguese by Rahul Bery

Inside the Coffer

Ioana Nicolaie

WHEN I WAS A young girl, I learned that at the edge of our country is a vast sea. Only, there's a transparent wall built around it and only one way out. Foreign ships dock there, fill their floating bellies and then leave again. The other edge of our country belongs to the river. Boats glide across it and I – a child of the northern mountains – used to imagine them on a trail of white paint, leaving a blackish paste behind them that was deadly to the touch. There is also another river to the West, the Mureş. More is known about this river because it's where people go to run away or die. Those that try to swim across are always shot.

As if he were two kinds of sturgeon – sevruga and sterlet alike – a cousin of mine managed to slip beneath the waves unnoticed and emerge on the other side. Austria granted him exile, and, just like that, he was rich. I would have given the shirt off my back to be in his shoes. We all would. In a letter, he told us that he'd filled his fridge for the first time in his life, and with foods that we couldn't even dream of: different kinds of chocolate, tinned meat, cheese, sweetened yoghurt, which we didn't even know existed! There, in the other world, everyone wore jeans and branded trainers. They wore their jackets a few times and then gave them away.

Socks were disposable, just like everything else, which he listed because no one back home believed him. And the photos, we realised from the ones he sent, were always in colour, not in black and white, like ours.

I imagined our borders as increasingly impassable; great trenches over which no bridge could be built. As I grew older, these grooves got deeper and I began to realise that we were all living inside a trunk, a tightly sealed and empty box. At school, we were learning Russian because communism came to us from the East. We were also learning French, although I never heard of anyone ever going to France. As for English, only one of the five parallel classes at my school was lucky enough to study it. If that language could have somehow turned into wings, the whole class would have flown over the ocean to America in a heartbeat.

You don't have, or need, much in the trunk: some words and patriotic songs, the fluttering flag and bits and pieces of food. You don't need television: the two-hour daily broadcast only covers the Party and the Beloved Leader. You have zero need for the radio: for ten years, they haven't played a single foreign song. On the walls of the trunk, they've drawn enormous windows so you can pretend to look outside; the sky has been painted blue overhead. Through these, you can see Russian astronauts (and the Romanian one, Dumitru Prunariu) lift off into outer space.

When the Revolution broke out in December 1989, splits and cracks in the trunk started to show. The helicopter bearing the country's dictator, Nicolae Ceaușescu, struck the trunk's padlock and was forced to land. The streets were filled with fear, soldiers and tanks, and in the big cities the dead began to pile up. The television began to broadcast live, releasing made-up reports of insurgent terrorists and poisoned drinking water. Light exploded through millions of cathode-ray tubes onto black and white screens – blinding and so terrific that you couldn't tell that our spontaneous revolution was nothing more than a coup d'état. The dictator was judged within a few hours and executed on Christmas day.

The trunk had burst open deafeningly that winter; bare hands wiped away the painted windows, and the hopeless trenches around us began to knit their banks, like a wound healing. People reacted with inexpressible joy: only a mole emerging in broad daylight and *seeing* for the first time could understand it. We were free after nearly 50 years. It was as if we could finally recollect ourselves after so many lifetimes. My cousin in Austria decided to come home right away, but it would take another ten years before he was free to cross the border.

The ragged remains of the former trunk were swept aside when Romania joined the European Union in 2007. What no one saw, however, were the fragments buried deep beneath the dust; the parts that never really disappeared. The former dictator, a man who had killed hundreds of the Revolution's soldiers, hadn't really left us; he'd merely assumed a different form.

I was twenty-six when I left Romania for the first time, and I will never forget the afternoon when I arrived in Berlin. I remember writing to my parents about how the earth looked from the plane; it seemed endless, stretching out as far as the eye could see, without borders or cavernous ditches to be crossed. My cousin decided to leave again and find work in Italy. And my brothers took themselves to Spain and England. Millions of Romanians dispersed across the continent after years of prolonged captivity. They learned new languages, did low-level work, lived with difficulty, and, in some countries, were singled out by groups of extremists and considered dangerous. All of them dreamed of returning home one day, for there was so much to be done in the former trunk. The initial attempts to rid the country of corruption had turned out to be nothing more than a botch job, and things arguably went from bad to worse.

Ceauşescu's cronies managed to stay in power for almost thirty years. The party had grown fat and swelled its ranks, wrapping itself in the flag. After countless trips to Moscow, it began stealthily to dig up members of the old guard, and instead of wilting, they began to flower right away, in increasing number. They were, in fact, viler than ever, engaged in various intimidation campaigns. Prominent intellectuals, writers and philosophers were taken apart on prime-time television, and the media began to smear truly free institutions, like the Romanian Cultural Institute, deliberately perverting their message.

Little by little, the truth was painted over, and once again the iron straps of the trunk began to tighten around us. Those not poisoned by corruption regarded it with horror. 'We were born in a dictatorship; we cannot afford another,' they all said. They filled the public squares again, they gathered in the cold and called for an independent judiciary. On 10 August 2018, I was suffocated – along with tens of thousands of other protesters – by tear gas scattered by riot police. In Sibiu, a city in the middle of the country, there has been continuous anti-corruption protests for over 500 days. The weeds that grew inside the old trunk continue to sprout, nevertheless. You rip them out it one place, but they pop up again someplace else. They have tremendous roots, multiplying like something out of a fairy tale. They block paths across borders and obscure the way we see the world from our windows. Reality becomes an outline, one without truth, completely misleading. In times like this, history slowly turns its back and, like Walter Benjamin's angel,[1] begins its recession into the future (*à rebours*) with enormous wings.

I was born inside a trunk, and I lived in it for almost fifteen years, believing that no one would ever be able to break it open. To the north there was a similar coffer, to the east another, and another still to the south. The rulers of the largest and most poisonous of these had been building walls between us and the rest of the world for half a century. When these walls finally fell, one after the other, Europe finally became a great, luminous expanse with a common sky. The walls were turned to rubble and sold as souvenirs; bringing together people who resembled each other, despite speaking different languages. And this new country slowly became more self-aware. It began to rediscover and rebuild itself. However, the weeds still pop up unexpectedly from time to time along one border or another. When people begin to forget or are no longer paying attention, you see them suddenly take root. And then the windows start to look like padlocks, just as they did in the past.

I've been a citizen of Europe for twelve years, and I'm proud of it. When I visit other continents, I wear my Europeanness around my shoulders like a cloak. I revel in its elegance, its civilised lines, its atypical beauty. I admire nothing more than the mixed cultures from which it arose. In the nineteenth century, the most beloved Romanian poet, the romantic, Mihai Eminescu wrote:

Past and future, ever blending
Are the twin sides of same page
New start will begin with ending
When you know to learn from age.

So, let's better understand the past so that we can see the future clearly. As for the present, we are all responsible for it. Under no circumstances should we allow ourselves to wear rose-tinted glasses. Truth, freedom, the rule of law, and respect for others are non-negotiable values. If we do not learn from the mistakes of the last century, we will find ourselves alone, without freedom or hope, enclosed between walls we ourselves have allowed to be built. We must, therefore, clear the smallest weeds remaining in the coffer, thoroughly, in east and west alike, so that they can never sprout again.

Translated from the Romanian by Jean Harris

Notes

1. In his ninth thesis on the Philosophy of History, Walter Benjamin equated Klee's 'Angelus Novus' to the Angel of History: 'It shows an angel who seems about to move away from something he stares at.... This is how the Angel of History must look. His face is turned toward the past. Where a chain of events appears before us, he sees one single catastrophe, which keeps piling wreckage upon wreckage and hurls it at his feet.'

Ride

Tereza Nvotová

HAVE YOU EVER BEEN on that awful fairground ride that slowly lifts you to the top of a huge, flashing tower? Once you're up there, all movement stops. All you can hear is the whistling of the wind. Your eyes can see far and wide. It feels as though you've been elevated above all earthly concern. Down below, people swarm as if in a frenzied anthill. And then, suddenly, you hurtle back towards the ground at a speed faster than the laws of physics would appear to permit. The cold steel sucks you all the way down, to rock bottom.

I'm sitting up here, looking down, and I want to get off. But I can't.

★

I'm staring at my computer screen. Tanks, armoured vehicles, burning streets, terrified civilians in clothes spattered with blood. My boyfriend comes home from the shop carrying a Ukrainian flag. We hang it from the balcony of our Prague flat. I wonder whether it's just a pathetic attempt at a woke gesture.

★

I'm on Skype with my sister. She's calling me from Moscow. She tells me about how the local shops are selling socks and towels with Putin's face on them, and about how the Russians are saying that Crimea is historically their territory, so what's the problem? Her 6-month-old son is wriggling in her arms. They're going to have to stay there for a couple more months and ride it out.

★

I'm sitting at a large glass desk, attending a grant committee hearing at the Slovak Film Fund. My hands are sweating. If the committee doesn't approve funding for my first film, I won't get to make it. I'm in the room with five older men.

'Tereza, dear, this is just a depressing story. Who wants to watch rape?'

'I don't know, but considering that one in three Slovak women have experienced sexual or physical abuse, I kind of think that people might be interested.'

'Why don't you make a film about how someone has sex for the first time instead? About the beauty of it, about the difficulty of overcoming shyness. You should really focus on the coital act itself.'

I don't know what to say.

★

It's 5 a.m. A new friend of mine is singing 'Walking on Broken Glass' at a Prague karaoke bar. I think I've fallen in love. But it doesn't matter. Tomorrow, he's going back home to New York.

★

World politicians are walking hand-in-hand down the streets of Paris. My mum is making soup. She can hear the telly playing in the background. 'Who's there?' she asks.

'Merkel, but also a few officials from Turkey, Egypt and Russia. For a freedom of speech march, this is some serious hypocrisy,' I reply.

The Slovak Prime Minister Robert Fico is also among the crowd.

A few days later, I find out that the Charlie Hebdo attackers shot the place up with guns they had bought legally in Slovakia.

★

Hi Jacob. How are you? How's New York? I've been so angry recently. I don't know if you've read about the Slovak truck full of dead immigrants that they found in Austria. They'd suffocated because the motherfucker at the wheel hadn't bothered to open the door since Serbia. And that's not even the worst part. My fellow citizens are celebrating their deaths on social media, and our MPs are writing racist blogs about how it's the immigrants' fault and how they deserved it. Fuck, man. This is sick.

★

I pull over at the Serbian border. I'm nervous. The van is packed full of clothes for refugees, which is illegal. It's forbidden to help. 'Cocaine, heroin, Kalashnikov?' asks the Serbian border guard. 'What?' I respond, confused. 'No, no drugs or guns,' my friend finally answers. The guard frowns, but he lets us through. We cross the border out of the European Union and enter the Wild East.

I'm walking alongside a metal fence. There are thousands of people, among them hundreds of children, crammed behind it. They're waiting for a bus to take them across the border. An elderly man hands me a 50-euro note through the wire mesh. 'Water! Buy water! Please!' Is he serious? After a while of asking around, I find out that nobody has given them any food or water for 24 hours. I storm off to the makeshift Red Cross storehouse. The employees are smoking and drinking coffee outside the entrance. All around, there are stacks of food, blankets and bottled water. I turn to the lady in the door and start yelling, 'Are you fucking kidding me? You are responsible for the food supply!'

She pushes back, arguing that it's dangerous for the employees to hand out food when there are so many immigrants out there.

'So you're just going to let them die instead?'

'We have our orders.'

When she turns around, I sneak into the storehouse and steal a pack of water and some blankets. On my way back to the camp, I send my group of independent volunteers into the storehouse to fetch more stuff. Soon the sun goes down. The bus that was supposed to come to pick up the barefoot children never came.

★

The sun is rising. The grips are offloading our equipment while some patients of a nearby Slovak psychiatric clinic, who are just having their morning cigarette, holler at us from the barred balconies. I enter the building and begin discussing the position of the camera with my DOP, when suddenly, the kids burst into the room. 'Hey, Tereza! Where's the catering? What time are we gonna start shooting? Can we fight in front of the camera afterwards? You want some crisps?' I introduce the kids to the actresses playing the lead roles in my film and leave them to get acquainted. After a while, the main protagonist walks over to me: 'Jesus, they're not kids at all! That Misha told me she knows exactly what our film is about, because her father used to rape her before she was sent to the orphanage.'

During the shoot, I never yell 'action'. I just give a slight nod to the actress playing the doctor. That way, the kids pay no mind to the camera. They just completely immerse themselves in playing out the situation they know so well – group therapy. The scene which we laboured over for so long while writing the script is coming alive before my eyes.

★

Hi Jacob. I'm sitting on the bus, finally getting back to Prague. So, I was shooting the Slovak elections till 3 a.m. today. Guess who's made it into Parliament? A real, full-blown Nazi who openly condones the deportations in WW2. He and his Nazi entourage got 8 per cent of the vote and won 15 seats. One in five Slovaks voted for him, and 25 per cent of first-time voters. Sometimes I question my role in society, whether I should make films and try to speak to people that way, or speak to them directly, or whether I should not bother speaking at all.

★

I'm looking at my dead uncle lying in a clear-view casket. There's a row of people I don't recognise standing next to it. One by one, they walk up to my uncle, whisper something in his ear and touch his face. Should I also do that? I never used to touch his face when he was alive. Why do it when he's dead? Suddenly, the organ comes alive with a thunderous roar, and the requiem begins. About thirty priests process into the scene. My uncle was a priest himself, so he's getting a 'special' funeral. The clerics serve the whole mass in unison. Same gestures, same words. I feel like I'm in some kind of strange dream, but I know that he would've enjoyed it. He liked a bit of a show. What he didn't like was the Slovak church with its hypocritical priests who had collaborated with the communist secret service and divulged confessional secrets for money. I think about how he emigrated. The family were utterly mystified when, one day, he didn't come back from holiday in

Yugoslavia. He only sent a letter once he had arrived in the Vatican. My mother wasn't allowed to study because of him. When my uncle returned after the Velvet Revolution, he was sent to work as a chaplain at the church of some former secret service agent. He couldn't take it and took off once more. When he became sick and destitute, the church couldn't have cared less. Now he's lying here, surrounded by people who preach in their churches that women should be categorically subordinate to men, that LGBT rights are the devil's work, and that all good people of faith should vote for the neo-fascists.

★

Brooklyn. I'm sitting on the windowsill in Jacob's flat and smoking. 'Purple Rain' is playing from the speakers. Prince has died. Jacob sits down next to me. He kisses me and tells me about how he broke up with his ex. She wanted to have a family and he didn't. Do I want a family? I don't know. I can't imagine the kind of world that my children would live in. Diminishing water supplies, mass migration, natural disasters… I don't believe humankind will manage to save the planet from climate catastrophe, let alone from the economic crisis that's bound to follow. 'I think I'd rather adopt a child. Why make new kids when there are so many that no one wants?' I tell Jacob. He smiles but doesn't say anything.

★

I'm standing nervously in a cinema corridor, watching people file out of the theatre. Many come over and congratulate me on the successful premiere. Suddenly, my father's brother embraces me. Unexpected. He quietly thanks me. He's finally understood why his daughter was acting so strange all throughout puberty. She'd probably been raped. It's a shame he's only realising it now. But better late than never, I guess.

I'm sitting on the toilet, reading a review of my film in the Slovak mainstream press.

> With her film, the director levels a passionate indictment. But at whom? At men, for having penises? It's no secret that, despite millennia of civilisational progress, our world is still but a jungle where the strong do as they will and the weak suffer as they must. Anyone who is timid and quiet, who has not learnt to stand up for themselves, and to say a resolute and resounding NO – whether it be a woman, a child, or a whole society – is asking for trouble.

I'm sickened. But then I console myself, thinking that this is exactly the kind of attitude that made me want to make the film.

★

February 2018. Lunch party on Hollywood's Sunset Boulevard. I'm ordering salad. There are about fifteen TV screens around. I'm introduced to the focus puller who worked on my favourite childhood film, *E. T.*. He tells me about how Spielberg used to play videogames with the child actors during the breaks. Suddenly I look up. All the TV screens are showing the same scene: kids filing out of a school with their hands above their heads. The headline reads that seventeen people have been killed in a shooting. Parkland. The party goes on. It seems like nobody's paying any attention to the news. 'God, what's happened?' I ask. 'Ah, some school shooting again,' says the focus puller. 'What? Is nothing ever gonna change here with the gun laws?' I ask. 'Well, it's in our Constitution. You can't change that.' Suddenly I feel proud to be a European. This would never happen at home.

One morning, a few days later, I wake up to the chime of my phone. A journalist and his fiancée – Ján Kuciak and Martina Kušnírová – have been shot in Slovakia. It was only recently that I visited his editorial office and saw him sitting there.

★

I'm holding a candle, standing by the stage and looking up at the Slovak President. He isn't saying anything, just holding a moment of silence for Ján. I can see my breath. It's almost fifteen degrees below freezing, but even so, there are about 25,000 people standing in the square with me. Next time, 65,000 will show up. And then once again after that. These are the largest protests that Slovakia has seen since the Velvet Revolution.

The whole country is plastered with hoardings reading: 'THE MAFIA WILL NEVER OWN SLOVAKIA!' Many of us crowdfunded to have them made. I'm standing on the stage and yelling into the microphone. 'I am ashamed for my country, where people get shot for telling the truth! I am ashamed for Prime Minister Fico and Interior Minister Kaliňák, who have sold our country to murderers! I am ashamed for all of us, who for so long have stood idly by while the people in power have been destroying our freedom and dismantling our democracy! But I am standing here nevertheless because I still have faith that in the end, truth will prevail!' The people clap and chant.

As I walk off the stage, I wonder whether I really believe what I just said. Will truth prevail? What if it doesn't?

According to one philosophical theory of persistence, in order for an object to persist from one moment in time to another, the object from the earlier time must be the same object found at a later time.

They didn't teach us the theories of persistence in

school. We were taught that humanity marches ever forward, and that Europe is always progressing. But what if we have been on this mad, dizzying ride for centuries, simply going up and down, and round and round? What if Europe remains the same as always, swinging between periods of conflict and strife and periods of peace and progress? We scale the cold, neon mast and then drop back down, again and again and again. But each time we climb to the top, our cheeks gently caressed by the breeze, we forget about our previous fall.

Slovakia only began to wake up following the tragic murder of a young journalist and his fiancée. We have since elected our first woman president, who has spent her life fighting against corruption and for the environment. Did we need to fall in order to bounce back up?

Hindus believe that the universe is governed by three deities: Brahma, the creator; Vishnu, the protector; and Shiva, the destroyer. The latter's role is to obliterate the universe so that it may be built anew. The destroyer is, at the same time, the transformer. According to Hindus, Shiva's destructive power is not ill-purposed. It is simply a catalyst for necessary change.

Over the last few years of my chaotic quest to change things for the better, I have understood that a single gesture of goodwill isn't enough; that my isolated actions, manifestos and social media posts are not really helping anyone. Europe requires far more than that, because evil will always come back in one form or another. Europe requires *persistence*.

In fact, it's precisely thanks to their *persistence* that populists, criminals and fascists are reclaiming power in Europe. It's because of the *persistence* of anonymous individuals labouring at their computers that people today have increasing faith in malign conspiracy theories. *Persistence* is a tool we – Europeans who value democracy, equality, freedom and human rights – lost while climbing up in the flashing amusement ride. We simply have to be present all the time. Because freedom is not and never has been a permanent status quo.

Translated from the Slovak by Jakub Tlolka

The Crisis of Trust

Renata Salecl

DURING ONE OF MY undergraduate lectures, I was deeply moved when almost a quarter of my students said that their best friend was a dog. When I asked them why, they told me that is was impossible to trust people these days, and that dogs are more honest and loving, always happy to see you when you come home.

Nowadays, we constantly hear how we cannot trust politicians, business leaders and various other experts. And when it comes to Europe, and the wider EU project, many seem to have both a lack of trust in its founding ideals and in the future of this cooperation. Here, too, countries do not seem to trust each other, and in the wake of Brexit, the burning question has become which country will abandon ship next, which country will turn against the Union, both politically and economically.

If it seems that the public distrust politicians and business leaders, the latter seem to trust ordinary people even less. Nowadays, governments are almost competing with one another to see who will use the most elaborate surveillance mechanisms, and businesses are unscrupulously collecting data about their consumers.

Even on an individual level, this mistrust in trust is leading to greater social control. The fact that people have less and less confidence in each other has prompted a significant expansion of the surveillance industry, allowing people to track and monitor each other. Some parents use video cameras to spy on babysitters; others are using computer software to check up on their children's nursery teachers. Partners are tracking each other's movements on their mobile phones; while the recording and monitoring of people at work is so prevalent that it is rarely challenged.

On a societal level, this obsession with surveillance has arguably led to the criminalisation of everyday life. At one time, an individual was considered innocent until proven guilty, but today the individual is considered an offender first, and then must prove their innocence. Some years ago, the late Norwegian criminologist Nils Christie wondered why crime in Norway had increased in the decades when living standards had significantly improved, and when the country itself was relatively peaceful, with few internal conflicts. Christie's answer was that ordinary Norwegians did not suddenly become major offenders; they had just begun to use new mechanisms to report crime. And as people were less likely to know those living next door, they became less trusting of each other. Minor transgressions, which before were dealt with within the community, were now being reported to the police. Let's say that there was someone stealing chickens in a small village. In the past, villagers would have caught the thief themselves; they might have punished them or – if it was someone that was normally a respectful member of the community – forgiven them for their crime. Today, of course, they would report such a thief to the police immediately. While there might have been as many chicken thieves in the past as today, the crime statistics suggest otherwise.

The reporting of crimes has another paradoxical connection with trust. If people were to ask whether they trust authorities – such as police or judges – they might say that they don't trust them at all, citing various miscarriages of justice. However, if something bad were to happen to these same people, they would call the police or go to court without a moment's hesitation. When the British philosopher Onora O'Neil explored the question of trust, she encountered precisely this duality. She found that people often choose to rely on those that they would otherwise describe as untrustworthy. For example, people say that they don't trust the food industry but will then buy all of their groceries from big supermarket chains. This difference between words and actions is particularly obvious in relation to doctors. When we are healthy, we often complain about unreliable doctors, but when we get sick we quickly turn to them for help.

Even more complications arise when it comes to the news. While claiming not to trust the media, many people still consume misinformation online through social media. It is not surprising that 'fake news' is such a problem these days, and that it often targets precisely those with doubts about traditional news sources. When Kellyanne Conway, the U.S. Counselor to President Trump, called the false statement about the number of people at Trump's inauguration 'alternative facts', she was actively trying to appeal to this demographic. No one would object to our right to question what is presented as truth. However, believing in fake statements as being just another form of truth annihilates trust in any source of knowledge or facts.

Another trust issue emerges when we consider big data. We often blindly consent to giving our data away when using various apps or browsing the internet. If we were to actually read the terms and conditions, I imagine we'd never download another app again, put on wearable technology or connect to open internet servers. The problem with informed consent is that it primarily protects the provider of a service, while for the consumer it is increasingly a forced choice. We can decide to either consent to giving away our data or not. But, if we refuse, then we lose out on being able to enjoy the device collecting the data. There is also a rather optimistic notion that the collection of this data will usher in progress and be beneficial for individuals and society at large. The cost of this belief, however, will be paid even more heavily by future generations. On top of issues around the mismanagement of data and new forms of surveillance, future generations will need to deal with the fact that they never consented to their data being collected from the moment of conception. This is why researchers dealing with the problems of big data warn that our ideas of privacy and informed consent do not encompass the fact that nowadays data on children is being collected on a massive scale without them being able to control or comprehend the impact this will have on their future lives.

People might feel that there is less trust in today's society, while at the same time willfully giving away their data to technology giants and on social networks. They might not have faith in their friends and neighbours, but will trust bots they encounter online, or anonymous reviews left on sites like TripAdvisor, despite them possibly being manipulated. Here it is wise to remember the words of the English writer Samuel Johnson that we are inclined to believe those whom we do not know because they have never deceived us.

This is also relevant when it comes to public opinion on scientists and doctors. Consider, for example, the anti-vaxxer movement; similar to other countries, in Slovenia some people who refuse vaccination are expressing distrust in the science behind it, but they have no problem believing random theories online about the dangerous side effects of vaccination. Here, too, people do not trust traditional authorities, doctors, for example, while they easily identify with anonymous anti-vaxxers online, embrace various forms of naturalism which refuse established medical treatment or believe in theories which science rejects.

One of the causes of this so-called 'truth crisis' is the change in the way people perceive community in these neo-liberal times, especially against a backdrop of heightened individualism and social media. While people choose to not put the good of the community before themselves, they expect others to do so. We, therefore, have a situation in which people do not think of themselves as part of the community, yet nonetheless imagine that such a community exists and that others believe in it. Similarly, some people may no longer believe in the EU project, but expect that others do, which is perhaps why they might not fear its collapse.

When Sigmund Freud pondered why people respect certain moral codes and follow the ideals of social justice, he concluded that an individual's behaviour is very much affected by their expectations about other people's behaviour. The basis of society, which relies on and upholds certain ideals of social justice, is that individuals limit their own behaviour, with the expectation that others will follow suit and limit theirs, too. An individual, therefore, tries not to do socially damaging things and expects that, in return, other people within the community will also not do them, and thus no harm is caused to the individual or the society at large. Individualism, in contrast, relies on a different perception of trust. Here, one follows the logic that an individual can make their own choice, while still expecting others to make a less selfish one. In this scenario, the wellbeing of the individual will be protected regardless of any extreme individualism.

With regard to Europe, we encounter a similar crisis of trust. A number of countries, and many individuals, behave as if they do not need to trust in the idea of the Union, while they nonetheless hope that others will. Similar delusion was at work during the Brexit vote in the UK when many Remainers didn't go to the polls, believing that enough of their compatriots would vote remain anyhow. And even some who voted leave did not necessarily identify with the idea of Brexit; thinking that remain would prevail, they just wanted to express their anger at politics and in general.

Trust in the EU today can neither rely on nostalgia for what was, nor on the idea that there is no alternative. Rather trust should follow the idea that it is possible to envision collaboration that allows for rethinking what form the Union will take. When we talk about the erosion of trust, we should not forget that trust is far less rational than we think. However, when we ponder whether or not to trust, it is worth remembering another saying by Samuel Johnson: 'It is better to suffer wrong than to do it and, happier to be sometimes cheated than not to trust.'

The Same Stone

Edurne Portela

IT'S THREE IN THE afternoon on one of the hottest days of the Madrid summer. I put on a light dress, a hat to keep off the sun, then grab my phone and house keys and head to a street called Mesón de Paredes, which is barely a hundred metres from mine. I walk along it from top to bottom, but there's no sign of what I'm looking for: a little bronze plaque fixed in the pavement, inscribed with a person's name I still don't know, the date of their birth, their exile, their deportation, the name of the concentration camp where they were imprisoned, the date of their death. I know it's on this street, but I walk up and down in the sweltering sun to no avail. I'm about to abandon my efforts, pondering the paradoxes of memory: when you go in search of it, it slips away, it resists, it doesn't materialise. But this is no weather for philosophising. I tell myself I'll try again another time, but then I get a message from my partner. He's found the exact address online: Mesón de Paredes 60. I've just walked straight past on the opposite pavement, in the shade, without seeing it. I go back and this time I do see it, glinting in the distance. I have to kneel to read it properly: 'Manuel García García, born 1915, exiled 1939, Stalag Trier, deported 1941, Mauthausen-Gusen, killed 3.7.1942'. I run my hand over it – you can barely feel a difference between the pavement and the plaque. At most, it would cause a passer-by the slightest of trips. In the next doorway, a group of young Senegalese guys with their bundles of handbags to sell in the street look at me and smile. Maybe they think I'm crazy, on my knees on the pavement, or maybe they know exactly what that commemorative cobblestone means.

It's not the only plaque like this in Madrid. A total of 449 will eventually be installed as part of the German artist Gunter Demnig's *Stolpersteine* project, which sets out to commemorate victims of Nazism and fascism on an international scale. '*Stolpersteine*' literally means 'stumbling stone'. I went to look for it, but many people will stumble upon it unexpectedly and come to know at least one of the thousands of Spanish Civil War exiles who escaped to France as Franco's troops advanced. On crossing the border, the exiles were detained and taken to French internment camps. Many were forcibly enlisted in the French army, others escaped and joined the resistance, and others (including women and children) were sent, on the instructions of Francisco Franco, by then the dictator, to concentration camps. Manuel García García was one of these.

We mark the anniversaries, we remember the dead, we shudder to this day at the untrammelled cruelty of genocides, we build museums and 'places of memory' that consign the victim's experience to a time that's finished, interpreted, closed off. When we remember the victims of fascism or Nazism, we focus on the horror and injustice of their death; we forget, however, that many of them were persecuted not for belonging to a particular ethnic community, but for defending political projects that aimed to transform the world they lived in. The '*Stolpersteine*' initiative in Madrid is laudable in that it preserves the memory of the fascist and Nazi horror and Francoism's complicity, but we also need to recover the memory of people's struggle and resistance in the face of that horror. This is why I welcome the release in Spain of the previously unpublished novel *Telefónica*, written by Ilsa Barea-Kulcsar in 1939 about her experiences in the Spanish Civil War. Perhaps, in Austria and other European countries, the author is known as Ilse Kulcsar for her work as a socialist activist in these places between the wars. In Spain, she has been known until recently as the 'wife of' Arturo Barea, a great writer who fought for the Spanish Republic during the Civil War, and whose autobiographical work, *The Forging of a Rebel*, translated by Ilsa Barea, is a landmark text in Spain's literature of exile. But Ilse was far more than this writer's wife and translator. She was a militant who twice went to prison, and who worked in the Spanish Republic's press and censorship bureau during the siege of Madrid, as well as a translator and writer. Ilsa Barea-Kulcsar is also a symbolic figure, representing the internationalist nature of anti-fascism and feminism which drew many women to participate actively in politics and the defence of democracy – women whom the spread of totalitarianisms in Spain and Europe condemned to exile, when not to imprisonment and death.

In a 1974 article for *Il Corriere della Sera*, Primo Levi wrote:

> Every age has its own fascism, and we see the warning signs wherever the concentration of power denies citizens the possibility and the means of expressing and acting on their own free will. There are many ways of reaching this point, and not just through the terror of police intimidation, but by denying and distorting information, by undermining systems of justice, by paralysing the education system, and by spreading in a myriad subtle ways nostalgia for a world where order reigned, and where the security of a

privileged few depends on the forced labour and the forced silence of the many.[1]

Our age also has its own fascism. All the signs Levi recognised in 1974 are present today, and yet we remain incapable of halting the advance of the far-right in Europe, or even of fighting the growing normalisation of its discourse, though we recognise it all too well. Because it is none other than a reification of that force which sent millions of people to their deaths, and which now, as then, centres on the demonisation of the different. Today the 'others' are immigrants, LGBTI communities, Muslims, feminists. Anyone who opposes the interests of the far-right is immediately labelled unpatriotic. This is how the far-right justifies its calls for increased State power and clampdowns on freedom of expression and the press, human and civil rights and judicial independence (as we see in Poland, Hungary or Turkey, where the nationalist far-right has reached power). Meanwhile, the European Union today is little more than its economic policies. Ever since its creation, it has charted a course based on economic interests that exclude or are incompatible with any show of solidarity with the most defenceless minorities, who are precisely the victims of the contemporary far-right.

Commemoration is necessary, but so is implementing memory policies that champion the struggle of men like Manuel García García and women like Ilsa Barea-Kulcsar against fascism; that show us the emancipatory and democratic current that swept through Europe, exposing those who would soon become executioners; and that remind us that allowing the normalisation of hate speech makes us all complicit. Perhaps then we won't stumble twice on the same stone.

Translated from the Spanish by Annie McDermott

Note

1. Primo Levi in *Il Corriere della Sera*, May 8, 1974; essay translated as 'The Past We Thought Would Never Return', in *The Black Hole of Auschwitz*, trans. Sharon Wood (New York: Polity Press, 2005), p. 34.

Everything I Have, I've Been Given

Karolina Ramqvist

ON THE MORNING I sit down to write this, a debate over Europe's future is raging. It is also the day after I finished my new book, a novel set in part in France during the 1540s, when white Christian men were defining modern Europe, setting off to explore the world and tame its wildness. My manuscript has been handed in and as far as this essay is concerned, I'm free to write what I like, but something from the past lingers. Or rather, someone.

I'm thinking about the most powerful woman in Europe at that time, the author Marguerite de Navarre, whose humanist writings were crucial in shaping Europe during the Reformation and the French Renaissance. She was a French queen and princess, and has been called the first modern woman. Upon reading this, I wondered what it meant and what it said about all the women who'd come before. Hadn't I read that Christine de Pizan, living over a century earlier and who is said to be the first woman to make her living as a writer, was the first feminist? In that case, what was the difference between a feminist and a modern woman?

As you can tell, I wasn't really used to reading history. I

didn't have a particularly developed understanding of how it stretches out behind us and is constantly being rewritten. That all modern women aren't necessarily feminists had, however, long been clear to me. I'd often been reminded of this in my 25 years as a feminist writing in Sweden – at first, the idea was shocking, but in time I would make sure to always bear it in mind: Not all women are feminists, not all feminists are women and not all women are the same. Even in a comparatively equal society, women differ in so many ways that one can hardly speak of 'women' beyond the biological denotation. It's a little different now than it was back when I started writing. Today it seems all Swedish women identify as feminists. Being a feminist has become praiseworthy; in certain contexts, it's a requirement even. Feminism has 'spread' in a way that those of us who came out as feminists in the 1990s were told it never would. We were informed it was a matter for the very few. We were called 'media feminists' by non-feminists and by older feminists whose fight on behalf of women had taken place inside academia or through activism, and it was said that we didn't know a thing about real women.

I'm not going to say that it was hard. In my lifetime it has never been particularly hard for a middle-class Swedish woman to be a feminist. It has been tiring and lonely on occasion, exposing and unpleasant even, but still comparatively easy. Now when I visit other countries and participate in conversations with readers and other authors I'm embarrassed by the question of what I've done to bring about equality. My answer is always the same: I haven't done a thing. The freedom and equality I have has been given to me by women from previous generations, and being a feminist today has meant that I am forever looking back at what they achieved while feeling incredibly grateful over my enormous luck as far as being in this time and place.

Marguerite de Navarre lived in France between 1494 and 1558. As an author and a debater, she focused on women's freedom but also on matters of religion, because those were the issues of the time and because they didn't interest her brother, King Francis I, whom she had been raised never to compete with. Like him, she became a great patron of the arts, a defender of the word, the arts and humanist ideals. In her court, she offered asylum to intellectuals such as Erasmus of Rotterdam, Jean Calvin and François Rabelais. One of Rabelais' novels, which is often said to be the most central work in humanism, is dedicated to her. He asks her to descend from her lofty perch for a moment – her 'eternally divine manor' – in order to partake in the more worldly affairs in his book. I knew this sentiment so well, from art, culture, and political debates: how a woman is asked to step down from her pedestal to the slightly realer reality the man knows. This is my interpretation: there is a notion of inherent loftiness that has always been used to ridicule or reproach those who deviate from masculinity but still want to assert their right, as though power becomes reprehensible when it is in a woman's hands. But perhaps I shouldn't be too sure of what Rabelais was saying. Reading five-hundred-year-old works is no easy task.

In a post-feminist era, many find it irritating when women whose lives predate feminism are called feminists or proto-feminists, and that's understandable, but the reverse remains a bigger problem: how women's political and intellectual deeds have been trivialised to the degree that today we can't catch sight of them. Marguerite De Navarre was one of the sources for the driving narrative of my book, and in working on it I have been able to see how she has – and has not – been read through time. The short story of hers that I referenced tells of a historical wrong committed by a French viceroy against a young orphaned woman, and the collection in which it is found is saturated with this ever-topical theme of men's violence against women. However, in the literary encyclopedia I consulted, these short stories are described as 'romantic historiettes' written first and foremost to entertain her brother Francis I and to honour the Italian Renaissance author Boccaccio.

That didn't sound particularly enticing. My book project was based on independent research using primary sources, and one reason I sought out the 16th century was because I'd started to feel like a stranger in my own time, but it soon became clear that I was suffering from one of my time's most common afflictions: I'd become one of those people who, rather than read for myself, was relying on brief online summaries. It was only when I engaged with the literary scholarship that re-evaluates Marguerite de Navarre, from Simone de Beauvoir to Patricia Cholakian, that her body of work began to open itself to me. Again, I had to seek out the work of previous generations, and again, I benefited from their labour. Twentieth-century research showed that de Navarre's short 'romantic' stories were in fact groundbreaking in how they contended with the representation of women as either temptresses or saints, describing subordination from a female character's own perspective and ditto violence from the perpetrator's, for the purpose of investigating the male psyche.

In the encyclopedia of literary history I found on the web, however, Marguerite de Navarre is described as amateurish, that is, as someone who loved literature but could never create anything of note herself. This conjured the image of a queen who took to writing as she would have taken to any other diversion. I had also fretted over the fact that the 16th-century women I was studying were all connected to the royal family, even though I knew that 'regular' women's stories simply weren't available to me because they didn't count. In fact, non-royal women weren't even counted for inclusion in the national registry. Furthermore, Marguerite de Navarre's works clearly show how the gender hierarchy cut through every other hierarchy. Women belonging to the higher nobility were used as currency in Europe's political game and their own opportunities to exert influence were directly related to their personal relationships with men. Marguerite de Navarre had to subordinate herself to her brother, including marrying the men he chose for her for the good of the country, in order to help him stay in power. Her own status was wholly dependent on his.

I once saw a painting of the poet and author Christine de Pizan, a miniature that shows her giving one of her books to another woman. It turns out that this motif recurs in depictions of Marguerite de Navarre as well. I imagined that these works moved in a particular historical space for women, a women's fold, and I fretted about this as well. I also recognised the image: the idea that a woman's writing only concerns other women and isn't really considered part of the real world. This was the kind of dark martyr-like thinking that would sometimes befall me. And it's true that many of Marguerite de Navarre's religious works, upon publication, were condemned by society because of how they propagated a more personal faith, beyond the compulsory rites and sacraments of the Catholic Church. It's also true that they were read and disseminated by women in the courts of other European countries, but in this way they also became instrumental to social development. Marguerite de Navarre's most controversial books were central to the new Protestantism in Europe.

When I finally started reading her properly, I felt so naive for having bought those early summaries wholesale and for not having been able to see how the way in which she was being remembered was diminishing her. After all, conducting a critical reading of historiography is foundational to a feminist. So why hadn't I done that? To begin with, I thought it was because this approach was so obvious. I was suffering from my generation's well-known disinclination to touch upon the obvious in speech and writing – a position being put to the test today, when the modern ideals of freedom, equality, and democracy that took shape during the Renaissance and which had seemed so self-evident when we were growing up, aren't self-evident any more.

In retrospect, I can see it had something to do with how cosseted the feminist looking glass I had always used had become. For so long I'd wanted a gendered perspective to be unreservedly accepted, but now that it was happening I wasn't as inclined to employ it. An important critique against my generation of feminists was the media-critical analysis of how feminist discourse moved from the political and academic arenas to that of the media and had to subordinate itself to the rules of the media game. Today the debate has gone one step further, to social media. I should have been happy that it was now trendy to talk about what feminists – and proto-feminists – have wanted to talk about for hundreds of years, but instead I was suspicious of the commercial veneer of such self-evident feminist positioning. When everyone is a feminist, the main stated aim of feminism – the day when women are no longer subordinate to men and the movement can disband – seems very far away.

The freedom and equality I have been given arrived slowly, in the shape of social reform meant to improve the lives of everyone, not just women. In Marguerite de Navarre's time, religious conflict was what was tearing Europe apart, but the idea of something grand and unworldly in the feminine and in feminism was the same as in later years. Today, when the conflict lies between openness and closedness, and Europe is again being defined by its view of unity and of people in the rest of the world, progressives are back being accused of belonging to a lofty elite, that is to say, a gang whose theories are irrelevant. Marguerite de Navarre was devoted to what became feminism's task in the 20th century: turning women into people. In the same way that we're not saying much when we say that we are women today, we're not saying much with the word 'feminist' either. But some of feminism could have been renewed and kept relevant by broadening the analysis of power so as to include more than just gender. At present, there are probably many of us who sense that precisely such a willingness and ability to see people as people is crucial to our future, but if and how this humanist and feminist inheritance will be used remains to be seen. I wonder how those who come after me will view what we are doing today and if those who engage with its representations will be willing to draw their own conclusions.

Translated from the Swedish by Saskia Vogel

A Tale of Two Witches:
Re-weaving a Social Europe

Hilary Cottam

SOMETIMES I THINK ABOUT witches. And I'm not alone. One morning, high above the train tracks near where I live in South London, a new message appeared. '*The witch is dead, but spell remains,*' it shouted in enormous, spooky white block letters. The witch in question was called Margaret and her spell was the neo-liberal promise that free, unfettered markets would bring wealth to all.[1] 'There is no such thing as society,' she pronounced. 'There are individual men and women, and each is in charge of their destiny.' What matters, she told us, was *efficiency*: everything that is important is visible, can be measured, and then managed for the better.

When I was younger, I left Britain, in large part to escape this spell. I wanted to find places with other ideas about society, people with different ways of thinking about and creating social change. And so, by coincidence, I met another witch. Her name was Maria: her skin was dark and dry like a wrinkled tamarind pod, and she barely came up to my waist. Maria was formidable and, in truth, more than a little frightening. She said she wanted to teach me. '*Ay Hilar, Hilar*' she intoned, beckoning me into the heady gloom of the small room where she lived and worked. 'I am the one who has the skills, look at me and write down what I tell you.' Intimidated, I agreed to weekly training with Maria and took notes as she drove her points home, with a hefty thump to my upper arm and a resounding spit to the floor.

Maria described herself as being in the 'healing' business. Her trade was remedies for what she called 'a clash of consciences': the disputes, anxieties and disease that grow from living cheek by jowl with things you cannot have. She understood the disquiet of living close to expensive, gleaming places you must clean and service but where you can never afford a home. She understood the angry frustration with formal systems of politics, where stories of better lives seem so far removed from personal reality. She understood the pain caused by inadequate health systems that cannot treat the complex physical and mental maladies that arise from the anguish of deep poverty; and the petty quarrels that start with neighbours when you live in cramped conditions and within systems that are unequal and unfair.

And perhaps I should have studied harder because today those deep divisions that were the stock-in-trade of Maria's business have become part of everyday life in Britain. We too are learning that anxiety produces divisions and ideas that are unthinkable in other times. Ideas that can neither be confronted nor assuaged with the usual tools of rational argument and considered debate. Ideas like Brexit.

The places where I work are Brexit places: Wigan, Rochdale, Swindon. These are places where the economies of a previous industrial revolution have been decimated, places where the spells of 'efficiency' have brought poverty not wealth, places where decent work is hard to find. But people who stand on the other side of this great national divide can find no logical answers to their questions: how could those who benefit most from European grants, those who will lose the few good jobs they have, how could 'those people' have voted to leave Europe? The answers perhaps lie in a different kind of thinking, or magic, if you will: one which understands that feelings and emotions matter as much as what is 'real'. That it hurts to live on the outside and the stories that are told of economic growth and opportunity are, for most people, little more than idle gossip which long ago lost its power to enchant.

The anthropologist Michael Taussig, who was very much concerned with magic and the state, wrote of 'pilgrimage as method', a way of hearing official and unofficial voices, a mode that allows us to witness and absorb, rather than explain.[2] I make my own pilgrimages to Wigan – a place for which I have much affection and where I began working a decade ago. Once the home of coal mining and industrial production, it is now a place where only the spell remains. There is work, but often the hours are long and the pay miserably low. And like almost everywhere in Britain, those who are poor are in work. Wigan council officials are inventive and they have come together with the community to find new ways to support one another. Food is rescued from the nearby landfill and in the holidays a team of community cooks produce thousands of meals for local residents. They feed children who, despite living in one of the world's largest economies, would otherwise starve. Wigan voted overwhelmingly for Brexit and all indications are that – if asked a second time – they would do so again.

Wigan, like the rest of Britain, is also experiencing the effects of a new technological revolution: one that is hollowing out communities whilst enabling a few to live with previously unimagined wealth. This revolution, based on digital technology, artificial intelligence and new forms of bio-technology, is presenting itself in ways we are struggling to understand. For some, the future seems bright, but others write of a dark form of auto-magic which is creating not only social and economic divides but also destroying the very possibility of democracy.[3] The seeds may have been sown decades earlier – the microchip was invented at the same time that Margaret was honing her spells – but now the effects are undeniable: changing our lives, our homes, our bodies and our communities at dizzying speed and in ways that no one individual can confront alone.

Many years ago, facing equally powerful forms of disintegration, our leaders dared to dream. Standing in the ruins of war and the devastation of the economic crisis of the 1930s they declared the need for a social revolution: for a new architecture that would spread the gains of their technological revolution – that of oil-based mass production – in new ways. There would be decent homes for all, health care, education, good jobs with unionised wages. Across Europe, the result was new forms of state welfare, a strengthened Union movement, and new forms of international collaboration from the birth of the United Nations to the genesis of what became the European Union.

In that era, to walk within bombed-out cities and witness the queues of desperate and hungry people, and to believe that within a short period of time Europeans would live in relative comfort, required if not magical thinking, certainly a huge leap of imagination. But politicians, activists, business leaders, intellectuals and artists came together around a collaborative social project. The result was an unprecedented era of social flourishing. Those lucky enough to be born in Europe were living longer, healthier, safer lives.

Today, these once-great social innovations no longer serve us. They cannot address the problems now confronting Europe: problems posed by the rapidly evolving nature of work, by deep demographic shifts, the challenges of living on a fragile planet and the growing inequalities in wealth and connection that are now deforming our societies. Our inherited social systems are a product of their time — mass industrial health systems were able to cure infectious diseases but they cannot confront modern conditions of the body and mind; schools that resemble assembly lines can instil the basics but they cannot equip us with the creative skills for continued learning that we require today. We face new forms of poverty that are as much about who we know as how much we have — our inherited systems cannot even recognise these problems, much less solve them.

Today we need our own social revolution. One that starts, not with commands from high above our heads but with *us* and with a new understanding of what it is to be wholly human. We must leave behind the mechanistic models of the last century and start instead with who we really are: people who are driven as much by a desire to connect and belong as by our individual goals. We need new forms of care and support and real possibilities to grow, and develop, our capabilities as individuals and communities, as nations and a continent. This revolutionary re-making will start by re-weaving the myths and stories of what is possible and joining together the existing radical experiences found in different pockets of our nations, glimpses of the future which are already around us.

What's the hardest thing about making change? Could it be the belief that a different way is possible? As the rain dripped through the holes in Maria's broken roof, she looked beyond, pointing to the stars. She never minimised the full scale of what was lost or missing in her or her neighbours' lives but at the same time she could see new connections: between place and economy, between people, between emotions and concrete reality — and she could weave these strands into alternative stories and possibilities.

We too can see our own points of light growing at the margins: new forms of work, of meeting, of making, protesting and debating, new forms of community.[4] But neither our political frameworks, nor our stories, have caught up and so we find ourselves tangled and trapped in spells that bind: stories that take our minds back to an imagined, glorious past rather than forward to what might be. To grow together we must create new stories, new spells and experiments that give birth to new possibilities. That is true magic.

Notes

1. Margaret Thatcher was Prime Minister of Britain from 1979 to 1990. In 2013 a version of *The Wizard of Oz* song 'Ding, Dong, the witch is dead' made a surprise entry into the British music charts marking Margaret Thatcher's death and continuing the protest against her policies and legacy.

2. Taussig (1997) *The Magic of the State*, Routledge London

3. See for example Zuboff (2019) *The Age of Surveillance Capitalism,* Profile Books London and Cadwalladr (2019) https://www.ted.com/talks/carole_cadwalladr_facebook_s_role_in_brexit_and_the_threat_to_democracy?language=en

4. Cottam (2019) *Radical Help: how we can re-make the relationships between us and revolutionise the welfare state,* Virago London

About the Contributors

Asja Bakić is a Bosnian poet, writer and translator. She graduated from University of Tuzla where she obtained a degree in Bosnian Language and Literature. Her debut poetry collection, *It Can Be a Cactus, as Long as it Stings* (2009) was nominated for a Kiklop literary award in 2010, and her short story collection, *Mars*, was shortlisted for the Edo Budiša Award for young writers. Asja has translated Emily Dickinson, Henri Michaux and Alejandra Pizarnik among others from English, French, German and Spanish into Croatian. She also writes a blog, *In the Realm of Melancholy* (asjaba.com), and is one of the editors and authors of *Muff* (muf.com.hr), a web page dedicated to feminist readings of popular culture.

Zsófia Bán is a Hungarian writer, critic and scholar. Her recent works include the novel, *Night School: A Reader for Grownups* (Open Letter Books, 2019), and *The Summer of Our Discontent* (Matthes und Seitz and DAADMarch, 2019), a book of essays exploring the visual representation of historical memory. Zsófia is the recipient of a number of prizes for fiction, essay writing and criticism, and was writer-in-residence with the DAAD Artists-in-Berlin Programme in 2015/16. She lives and works in Budapest where she is Associate Professor of American Studies at Eötvös Loránd University.

Annelies Beck is a writer and journalist. She has lived in the Netherlands, Brazil, the UK and Belgium. She read History at Ghent and obtained an MA in Brazilian Studies at ILAS, University of London. Annelies currently presents the daily current affairs TV programme *Terzake* at the VRT (Belgian public broadcasting), and is a regular contributor to various newspapers, including *De Standaard* and *De Morgen*. She is the author of *Across the Channel* (De Geus, 2011) which traces the plight of Belgian refugees in Glasgow during the First World War, and *Frenzy* (De Geus, 2019) which is set in Brazil.

Silvia Bencivelli is a science journalist, writer and radio/TV broadcaster. She has been working for RAI, the Italian national public broadcasting company, for fifteen years as a presenter on various programmes. She writes about science for various publications, including *La Repubblica, Le Scienze* and *Focus* and teaches Science Journalism at La Sapienza – University of Rome and at the University of Bari, as well as Communication and Science Journalism at several institutions. Her works include the novel, *My Witch Friends* (Einaudi, 2017), and the essays *Why We Like Music: Ear, Emotion, Evolution* (Music Word Media Group), *È la medicina, bellezza! – Perché è difficile parlare di salute* (with Daniela Ovadia, Carocci, 2016) and *Comunicare la scienza* (with Francesco Paolo De Ceglia, Carocci, 2013). Her latest essay is entitled *Sospettosi* (Einaudi, May 2019). She has received numerous awards for her work as a journalist and editor.

Hilary Cottam is an internationally acclaimed social activist whose work in Britain and around the world has focused on collaborative and affordable solutions to some of the greatest social challenges of our time, such as ageing, loneliness, chronic disease, good work and inequality. Hilary's book *Radical Help: How We Can Remake the Relationships Between Us*

& Revolutionise the Welfare State was published by Virago (Little Brown) in June 2018. She has been recognised by the World Economic Forum as a Young Global Leader and in 2005 was named UK Designer of the Year for her transformative social practice. Hilary's TED talk 'Social Services Are Broken' has had three quarters of a million views. Hilary continues to support communities and governments around the world to grow and extend an approach to social change which puts capability, relationships and deep human connection at its heart.

Lisa Dwan is an Irish performer, director and writer. She has worked extensively in theatre, film, and television, both internationally and in her native Ireland, and writes, presents, lectures and teaches regularly on theatre, culture, gender and Beckett. She recently starred in *Top Boy* (a TV series for Netflix produced by Drake & Lebron James), and in Harold Pinters' *The Lover & The Collection* at STC in Washington DC where she won the 2018-2019 Emery Battis award for outstanding contribution to acting. She is currently the 2018-2019 distinguished artist in residence at Columbia University where she is teaching at the Institute of Women and Gender studies and developing a new theatre piece with Colm Tóibín based on *Antigone* which will have its world premiere at The Gate Theatre in Dublin this November as well as new version of *Medea* which she is co-writing with Margaret Atwood.

Yvonne Hofstetter is a jurist and essayist who began her career in information technology. In 2001, Hofstetter joined EXE Technologies, a company that optimised the value chains of internationally active companies with the help of artificial intelligence. After a company merger in 2004, Hofstetter left and took over the management of the German branch of an Irish fintech company that specialised in algorithmic currency trading. On the occasion of the 2008-2009 financial crisis, a management buyout took place and TERAMARK Technologies GmbH was founded in the north of Munich, a cognitive assistance systems company that Hofstetter managed until 2019. Hofstetter is a sought-after keynote speaker on the subject of digitalisation. She has published, in German, the bestsellers *They Know Everything* (2014) and *The End of Democracy* (2016). Hofstetter received the 53rd Theodor Heuss Prize in 2018 for her democratic commitment and for her work on artificial intelligence with guard rails. Hofstetter lives in Freising near Munich, and in Vienna.

Nora Ikstena is a prose writer and essayist. She obtained a degree in Philology from the University of Latvia in 1992 and went on to study English Literature at Columbia University. She is a prolific author of biographical fiction, non-fiction, scripts, essays, and short stories. Her novel *Soviet Milk* is a national bestseller in Latvia and has been published in more than 20 countries. It was nominated for both the EBRD Prize and The Republic of Consciousness Prize in 2019. Nora is a member, and former chair, of the National Culture Council and a co-founder of the International Writers and Translators' House in Ventspils. In 2006, she received the prestigious Baltic Assembly Award, as well as the Three Star Order of Latvia.

Maarja Kangro has been described as one of the most formidable voices of her generation in Estonia. She has published six collections of poetry, four volumes of fiction and a book of essays, and has also written five opera librettos. Maarja has won numerous awards, among them, twice, the most important literature prize in Estonia, the Estonian Cultural Endowment's Literary Award (being so far the youngest author to have won the prize in the categories of both poetry and fiction). Her works have been translated into

15 languages, and she is herself a translator, translating mainly poetry and contemporary philosophy (among others Agamben, Vattimo, Leopardi, Zanzotto, Enzensberger). She currently lives in Tallinn.

Kapka Kassabova is the author of three narrative non-fiction books: *Street Without a Name* (Granta, 2008), *Twelve Minutes of Love* (Granta, 2011), and *Border: A Journey to the Edge of Europe* (Granta/Greywolf, 2017) which won the British Academy's Al-Rodhan Prize, the Saltire Book of the Year, the Stanford-Dolman Book of the Year, the Highland Book Prize, and was shortlisted for the US National Book Critics' Circle Award. Kassabova grew up in Sofia and as a young adult in the 1990s emigrated with her family to New Zealand where she studied French and Russian Literature and published her first poetry and fiction. Since 2005 she has lived in Scotland. Her native Balkans are the location for both *Border* and her new book, *To The Lake: A Journey of War and Peace* (Granta/Greywolf, 2020).

Sofia Kouvelaki is the Executive Director of the HOME Project. She was the Program Manager of the Bodossaki Foundation Program for Unaccompanied Minors and inter alia, in charge of projects on Social Welfare Provision to vulnerable groups. She has worked at the UN and at UNICEF in the economic analysis and social policy division and as an Adviser and Researcher for the public and private sector in Greece. She holds a Master of Science in International Political Economy from the London School of Economics and a masters degree in International Economics from Sciences Po, Paris. She has completed a Bachelor of Arts in Economics and International Relations at Brown University in the USA and a Certificate from the Harvard Program on Refugee Trauma and Recovery. Sofia has given talks and participated in panel discussions on unaccompanied minors and the refugee crisis in Greece, at the US Congress, Harvard University, Brown University, University of London (UCL), TEDx Athens, Building Bridges Film Festival, and many other institutions in Europe and the US. Sofia is currently based in Athens, Greece.

Carine Krecké is an interdisciplinary artist living and working in Luxembourg and Spain. She holds a PhD degree in Literature and Art from the University of Provence and a PhD in Economic Science from the Aix Marseille University. She regularly collaborates with her twin sister Elisabeth, (economist and artist), on artistic and non-artistic (legal, economic and social science) projects, which are often intertwined. Krecké relies on photography, drawing, painting, as well as literature (poetry, novels, plays, essays) to tackle issues such as mass surveillance, simulacra and voyeurism in our digital world. Over the past 15 years, Carine's work has been shown at numerous exhibitions and international events such as the European Month of Photography, Rencontres Internationales Paris-Madrid-Berlin, Paris-Photo, Drawing Now and Rencontres Internationales de Photographie d'Arles.

Caroline Muscat is an award-winning investigative journalist and the co-founder and editor of *The Shift News*, an online news portal launched in November 2017 as an investigative news outlet to address the gap in independent journalism in Malta. She was the former News Editor of *The Times of Malta* and *The Sunday Times of Malta*, the country's leading newspaper. Her main area of focus is corruption and human rights. She contributed to and co-edited the book, *Invicta: The Life and Work of Daphne Caruana Galizia*, a journalist assassinated in Malta in October 2017. As an activist, Muscat began her career at Greenpeace, where she was Regional Communications and Campaigns Director from 1999 to 2003.

Nora Nadjarian is a Cypriot poet and writer. She has won various international prizes, including the Commonwealth Short Story Competition, the Féile Filíochta International Poetry Competition and the Seán Ó Faoláin Short Story Prize. Her work concentrates on the themes of women, refugees, identity, exile, love and loss, as well as the political situation in Cyprus. She is best known for her short story collection, *Ledra Street* (2006), and has also featured in various international poetry and fiction anthologies, including *Being Human* (Bloodaxe Books, 2011), *Capitals* (Bloomsbury, 2017) and *The Stony Thursday Book* (2018). Her most recent works include *Selfie* (Roman Books, 2017) and *Girl, Wolf, Bones* (bilingual English-German edition, 2017).

Ioana Nicolaie graduated from the Literature Faculty of Bucharest University in 1997, where she also took a Master of Arts Degree in 1998. Her debut collection of poems, *Retouched Photograph* (Cartea Românească, 2000), was published following a competition. Her published work includes: *The North* (2005, nominated for the ASPRO Prize), *Faith* (2003, nominated for the Prize of the Bucharest Writers' Association), *Belly Heaven* (2005), *Cenotaph* (2006), and *The Adventures of Arik* (2008). In addition, she has written the text for an illustrated book about Bucharest. Her poetry has appeared in a number of anthologies in France, Britain, Canada, Bulgaria, the USA, Austria, and Sweden, including *Poésie 2003: Roumanie, territoire d'Orphée* (Théâtre Molière/Maison de la Poésie, 2003) and *New European Poets* (Graywolf Press, 2008). In 2008, Pop Verlag of Stuttgart published her collection *The North* in German translation. She is a member of the Romanian Writers' Union and PEN.

Bronka Nowicka is an interdisciplinary artist, a Doctor of Fine Art and a writer and a lecturer at the National Film School in Łódź. Her literary work has been published by Znak (Poland), Književna smotra, Sic (Croatia), Literatūra ir menas (Lithuania), Seedings (US), *Poetry Wales* and *Modern Poetry in Translation* (UK). She has presented her visual works, among others, at the Susanne Burmester Galerie in Germany, Trubarjeva Hiša Literature in Slovenia and Kunstnernes Hus in Norway. She has won the Nike Literary Award and the Złoty Środek Poezji (Golden Mean of Poetry) Award for her book *To Feed a Stone*. In 2017, she became a laureate of the New Voices From Europe project, carried out as part of the Literary Europe Live platform and offering support to outstanding European writers after their debuts.

Tereza Nvotová graduated in Direction from the FAMU film academy in Prague. Her feature debut *Filthy* has been screened at major festivals around the world including Rotterdam, Karlovy Vary, Cairo, and Santa Barbara. During its distribution *Filthy* took home more than 20 awards, making it one of the most successful Czech and Slovak films of the year. Tereza collaborates with various broadcasting companies, most notably HBO Europe which has co-produced her feature debut and two documentary films. Her latest HBO documentary *The Lust for Power* has been shortlisted for the European Film Academy Awards 2019. She is an alumnus of 2019 Berlinale Talents, and is currently working on her second feature, *The Nightsiren*, as well as the television mini-series *Convictions* based on the Cold War-era autobiography of Jo Langer.

Ana Pessoa is a Portuguese writer and translator living in Brussels. She has published three books for young adults: *Mary John, Supergiant* (White Ravens Catalogue, 2015) and *The*

Karate Girls' Red Notebook (Branquinho da Fonseca prize 2011). Ana's books are also published in Brazil, Colombia and Mexico. In her free time she writes biographical fiction, a blog (www.belgavista.blogspot.com) and participates in several writers' groups. Many of her stories have won awards in Portugal and abroad (Jovens Criadores 2013, Portugal; Castello di Duino 2011, Italy; Sea of Words 2010, Spain). Ana is one of the 39 emerging writers under 40 years old selected to participate in the European Children's Literature Hay Festival – Aarhus 39 in 2017.

Edurne Portela graduated in History from the University of Navarra and has a doctorate in Hispanic Literature from University of North Carolina. She is Professor of Literature at Lehigh University (Pennsylvania) and regularly publishes articles and essays as part of her research. Edurne has a Sunday column in *El País*, regularly participates in Radio Nacional de España and has collaborated with other media such as *El Correo/Diario Vasco* and *La Marea*. Her non-fiction works include *Displaced Memories: The Poetics of Trauma in Argentine Women Writers*. Her first novel, *Mejor la ausencia,* was published in 2017 and was awarded the 2018 Prize for the best fiction book of the year by the Gremio de librerías de Madrid. Her second novel, *Formas de estar lejos*, was published by Galaxia Gutenberg in 2019. Together with José Ovejero, she made the documentary *Vida y ficción* (2017).

Julya Rabinowich was born in St. Petersburg in 1970, but has lived in Vienna since 1977, where she also studied. She works as a writer and columnist, and also worked as an interpreter until 2006. She is the author of *Splithead* (2008), which won awards including the 2009 Rauriser Literaturpreis, *Herznovelle* (2011), nominated for the Prix du Livre Européen, and *Dazwischen: Ich,* her first book for children. Julya has been awarded the Friedrich-Gerstäcker Prize, the Österreichischer Kinder- und Jugendbuchpreis award and the Luchs Prize (*Die Zeit* & Radio Bremen), and one of her works was selected among the seven best books for young readers (Deutschlandfunk). In 2019, she published the children's book *Hinter Glas*.

Karolina Ramqvist is one of the most influential writers and feminists of her generation in Sweden. She has written five novels and is widely celebrated for her powerful explorations of contemporary issues such as sexuality, commercialisation, isolation and belonging. In 2015, Karolina was awarded the prestigious P.O. Enquist Literary Prize for *The White City* (*Den vita staden*), and for her 'unique and strong position in Swedish literature'. Her works include *It's the Night* and *Bear Woman* about a writer whose life becomes intertwined with the 16th century noblewoman, Marguerite de La Rocque, who survived harrowing years alone on a deserted island.

Apolena Rychlíková is a Czech filmmaker, journalist and publicist interested in social and political topics, particularly problems of inequality, housing, racism and gender. She graduated from FAMU (the Film Academy in Prague) and writes for the Czech left-wing website A2larm.cz, public radio and cooperates with Czech public TV. Her latest work *Limits of Work* was named Best Czech Documentary in the Czech Joy section at the 21st Ji.hlava International Documentary Film Festival. She has also won a prize for Best Opinion Journalism.

Renata Salecl is a philosopher and sociologist. She is Professor of Psychology and Psychoanalysis of Law at the School of Law, Birkbeck College, University of London and Senior Researcher at the Institute of Criminology at the Faculty of Law in Ljubljana, Slovenia. She is also Recurring Visiting Professor at the Cardozo School of Law in New York.

Her latest book, *Tyranny of Choice* (Profile, 2011), has been translated into 15 languages and was featured at TED Global. Her previous books include: *The Spoils of Freedom: Psychoanalysis and Feminism After the Fall of Socialism* (Routledge 1994), *(Per) versions of Love and Hate* (Verso, 1998), and *On Anxiety* (Routledge 2004). Her forthcoming book is *Passion for Ignorance* (Princeton UP, 2020). Salecl has also published numerous articles on contemporary art, among them catalogue essays on Jenny Holzer, Anthony Gormley and Sarah Sze.

Leïla Slimani is the first Moroccan woman to win France's most prestigious literary prize, the Prix Goncourt, which she won for *Lullaby*. A journalist and frequent commentator on women's and human rights, she is French president Emmanuel Macron's personal representative for the promotion of the French language and culture. Born in Rabat, Morocco, in 1981, she lives in Paris with her French husband and their two young children.

Janne Teller is a critically acclaimed and best-selling Danish novelist and essayist of Austrian–German family background. She has received numerous literary grants and awards, including the prestigious American Michael L. Printz Honor Award for literary excellence and the Danish Drassow's Literary Peace Prize. Her literature, which confronts philosophical questions in life and civilisation and often sparks controversial debate, is today translated into 30 languages. Janne Teller has published six novels, including the modern Nordic saga *Odin's Island* about political and religious fanaticism, as well as the existential *Nothing* that after initially being banned, is today considered a new classic by many critics. Her book, *War – What If It Were Here,* about life as a refugee, is adapted by the author to each country where it is published. Janne is also a human rights activist, and was one of the initiators of the 2013 Writers

Against Mass Surveillance campaign. She is a member of the jury of the prestigious German Peace Prize. She has lived and worked with conflict resolution and humanitarian affairs for the EU and UN in Mozambique, Tanzania and many other countries around the world.

Saara Turunen is an internationally acclaimed and award-winning author, playwright and director. Much of her work examines the themes of art, identity and social norms. Turunen is known for her two highly acclaimed novels, *Love/Monster* (2015) and *The Bystander* (2018), but also for her work in theatre. Her plays have been translated into numerous languages and performed all around the world. Turunen was awarded the Helsingin Sanomat Literature Prize in 2015, and the Finland Prize in 2016, both high-profile awards given annually in Finland.

Žydrūnė Vitaitė's experience includes business development and operations in technological companies, as well as management and leadership roles both in business and NGOs. She is president of AIESEC Lithuania, implementing projects on sustainable NGO development and youth leadership education, and Head of Sales at the engineering company ELDES. Žydrūnė is also the co-founder of Women Go Tech – the first mentorship program in Lithuania to encourage women to choose a career in ICT and engineering. The program is patronised by the President of Lithuania, Dalia Grybauskaitė, and supported by various other international corporations (www.womengotech.lt). She has developed numerous local and international conferences, and regularly speaks at global events (including the WEF Annual Meeting in Davos 2018, OSCE conferences, WPL Gathering in Lithuania) on topics of women's empowerment, gender equality, women in tech, men's role in gender parity, community building and youth engagement.

Gloria Wekker is an Afro-Surinamese Dutch anthropologist and writer. She is Professor Emerita in Gender Studies, Faculty of the Humanities, at the University of Utrecht. One part of her research focus has been the study of gender and sexuality in the Afro-Caribbean region and diaspora, while another important theme has been the ways that race still structures life in the Netherlands after 400 years of colonial rule. Among her publications is *The Politics of Passion; Women's Sexual Culture in the Afro-Surinamese Diaspora* (Columbia University Press, 2006), for which she won the American Anthropological Association's Ruth Benedict Prize (December 2007). More recently, she wrote *White Innocence; Paradoxes of Colonialism and Race* (Duke University Press, 2016), to much critical acclaim.

About the Translators

Rahul Bery is based in Cardiff and translates from Spanish and Portuguese to English. His translations have appeared in *The White Review*, *Granta*, *Freeman's*, *Words without Borders* and elsewhere and his first full-length translation, of David Trueba's *Tierra de Campos*, will be published in 2020 by Weidenfeld & Nicolson. He was the British Library's translator-in-residence for 2018-2019 and is currently working with the Stephen Spender Trust on developing resources for creative translation activities in classrooms.

Jen Calleja is a writer and literary translator from the German. Her poetry collection *Serious Justice* (2016) was published by Test Centre and her short story collection *I'm Afraid That's All We've Got Time For* is forthcoming in 2020 from Prototype. Her translations have appeared in *The New Yorker*, *The White Review* and *Granta*, and she has been shortlisted for the Man Booker International Prize and the Schlegel-Tieck Prize for her translations.

Ruth Clarke is a translator from Italian, French and Spanish. She has translated work by authors from Benin to Venezuela, including Mariana Enríquez, Cristina Caboni, Enoh Meyomesse and Leonardo Padrón. Ruth was a mentor for the British Council's Translation Fellowship and is keen to bring translation to the public stage, speaking at events such as Crossing Border Festival, London Book Fair and International Translation Day. She promotes translation as a panellist for New Spanish Books and 12 Swiss Books, and she is a founding member of The Starling Bureau, a London-based collective of literary translators.

Jennifer Croft won the 2018 Man Booker International Prize for her translation from Polish of Olga Tokarczuk's *Flights*. She has also received NEA, Cullman, PEN, Fulbright and MacDowell fellowships and grants, as well as the inaugural Michael Henry Heim Prize for Translation, the 2018 Found in Translation Award and a Tin House Scholarship for her creative memoir *Homesick*, originally written in Spanish, out now in English from Unnamed Press.

Katy Derbyshire was born in London and has now lived in Berlin for over twenty years. She translates contemporary German literature including Man Booker-nominated Clemens Meyer, Olga Grjasnowa, Heike Geissler and Christa Wolf. Katy also co-hosts a translation lab in Berlin and the bimonthly Dead Ladies Show, complete with its own podcast.

Born in Riga, poet and translator **Margita Gailitis** emigrated to Canada as a child. Gailitis returned to Riga in 1998 to work at the Translation and Terminology Center as part of a Canadian International Development Agency initiative. Today Gailitis focuses her energy on literary translation, having translated some of Latvia's finest poetry, prose and dramaturgy. In 2011 Gailitis was awarded the prestigious Three Star Order by the President of Latvia for work on behalf of Latvian writers. Gailitis' own poetry has been widely published.

Jean Harris is a novelist, translator and essayist based in Bucharest, Romania. She has been the 2007–2008 winner of the University of California's International Center for Writing and Translation grant for her translation of Ştefan Bănulescu's *Mistreţii erau blazi*. Her translations have appeared, among other places, in *The Guardian, Words Without Borders, Habitus* and jewishfiction.net. Harris holds a PhD in British and American literature from Rutgers University.

Emily Jeremiah is a professor at Royal Holloway, University of London, and the author of three academic books. She is also an award-winning translator of poetry and fiction. With her Finnish mother Fleur Jeremiah, she has co-translated five novels, one of which, Aki Ollikainen's *White Hunger* (Peirene Press), was longlisted for the Man Booker International Prize 2016. She has published two selections of translated poetry, by Eeva-Liisa Manner and Sirkka Turkka, with Waterloo Press. She holds an MA in Creative Writing from Goldsmiths, University of London, and her debut work of fiction, the novella *Blue Moments*, is forthcoming with Valley Press.

Annie McDermott's published and forthcoming translations from Spanish and Portuguese include *Empty Words* and *The Luminous Novel* by Mario Levrero, *Feebleminded* by Ariana Harwicz (co-translation with Carolina Orloff), *Loop* by Brenda Lozano, *Dead Girls* by Selva Almada and *City of Ulysses* by Teolinda Gersão (co-translation with Jethro Soutar). McDermott also edits books for Charco Press and reviews for the *Times Literary Supplement*. She has previously lived in Mexico City and São Paulo, Brazil, and is now based in London.

Julia Sherwood is a translator and literary organiser. She translates fiction and non-fiction from and into Slovak, Czech, Polish, Russian and English. She is based in London and serves

ABOUT THE TRANSLATORS

as the editor-at-large for Slovakia for *Asymptote*, the online journal for literary translation. In 2019 she received the Pavol Országh Hviezdoslav prize for translating and promoting Slovak literature in the English-speaking world.

Sam Taylor is a novelist, translator and journalist. He was born in England, spent eleven years in France, and now lives in the United States. His four novels have been translated into ten languages, and one of them – *The Republic of Trees* – made into a film. His translations from French include Laurent Binet's *The Seventh Function of Language* and Hubert Mingarelli's *Four Soldiers*, both of which were longlisted for the International Booker Prize, Maylis de Kerangal's *The Heart*, which won the French-American Translation Prize and the Lewis Galantiere Award, and Leïla Slimani's best-selling *Lullaby*.

Jakub Tlolka is an author, editor, and literary translator based in Bratislava, Slovakia. Though trained as a brooding political theorist, he currently specialises in the much more uplifting area of script translation, while occasionally doing scholarly translations to get his academic fix. He has worked on a number of critically acclaimed Slovak films and also heads an international conference and publishing platform devoted to promoting original student research in the humanities and social sciences.

Jim Tucker is a former classical philologist who translates into English from French, German, Italian and Hungarian, and also repairs vintage wristwatches. After making the acquaintance of George Konrád, he resolved to learn Hungarian in order to translate Konrád's essays. Since then, he has translated two of Konrád's novels (published together as *A Guest in my Own Country*, winner of a 2008 National Jewish Book Award), many of his essays and, more recently, work by

Zsófia Bán and other modern authors. He is currently completing an anthology of Transylvanian Hungarian poetry. He lives in Budapest with his dogs.

Rimas Uzgiris is a poet, translator, and critic. He is the author of *North of Paradise* (Kelsay, 2019). He is translator of *Caravan Lullabies* by Ilzė Butkutė (A Midsummer Night's Press), *Then What* by Gintaras Grajauskas (Bloodaxe), *Now I Understand by Marius Burokas* (Parthian), *The Moon is a Pill* by Aušra Kaziliūnaitė (Parthian), and *Vagabond Sun* by Judita Vaičiūnaitė (Shearsman). Uzgiris holds a PhD in philosophy from the University of Wisconsin-Madison, and an MFA in creative writing from Rutgers-Newark University. Recipient of a Fulbright grant, a National Endowment for the Arts Translation fellowship, he teaches translation at Vilnius University.

Saskia Vogel is a writer and Swedish-to-English literary translator from Los Angeles and based in Berlin. She has translated works by Johannes Anyuru, Karolina Ramqvist, and Lina Wolff. Her debut novel *Permission* (Dialogue/Coach House), a story of love, loss and BDSM, was published in four languages in 2019.

Jennifer Zoble translates Bosnian, Croatian, Serbian and Spanish-language literature. Her translation of the short story collection *Mars* by Asja Bakić was published by Feminist Press in March 2019. She received a 2018 grant from the New York State Council on the Arts for her translation of *Zovite me Esteban* ('Call me Esteban') by Lejla Kalamujić. She's an assistant clinical professor in the interdisciplinary Liberal Studies program at NYU, co-editor of 'In Translation' at *The Brooklyn Rail*, and co-producer of the international audio drama podcast Play for Voices.

About the Project

Hay Festival Europa28 brings women writers, artists, scientists and entrepreneurs – one from each of the 28 member countries – together to deliver their visions for the future of Europe. Part of the Wom@rts project, co-funded by the Creative Europe Programme, it represents a multi-disciplinary snapshot of the best minds of our time. In 2020, their work is shared through a new anthology, *Europa28: Writing by Women on the Future of Europe*, and at Hay Festival events around the world, including Hay Festival Europa28 in Rijeka 2020 – European Capital of Culture, Croatia.

Resist: Stories of Uprising

Edited by Ra Page

'A wonderful collection of stories about the enriching beauty
and strength of protest. A book to inspire us all.'
— *Maxine Peake*

At a time that feels unprecedented in British politics — with unlawful
prorogations of parliament, casual race-baiting by senior politicians,
and a climate crisis that continues to be ignored — it's easy to think
these are uncharted waters for us, as a democracy.

But Britain has seen political crises and far-right extremism before,
just as it has witnessed regressive, heavy-handed governments. Much
worse has been done, or allowed to be done, in the name of the
people and eventually, those same people have called it out, stood up,
resisted.

In this new collection of fictions and essays, spanning two millennia
of British protest, authors, historians and activists re-imagine twenty
acts of defiance: campaigns to change unjust laws, protests against
unlawful acts, uprisings successful and unsuccessful — from Boudica
to Blair Peach, from the Battle of Cable Street to the tragedy of
Grenfell Tower. Britain might not be famous for its revolutionary
spirit, but its people know when to draw the line, and say very clearly,
'¡No pasarán!'

*Featuring: Julia Bell, SJ Bradley, Jude Brown, Lucy Caldwell, Steve
Chambers, Martin Edwards, Uschi Gatward, Luan Goldie, Gaia Holmes,
Nikita Lalwani, Zoe Lambert, Anna Lewis, Irfan Master, Donny O'Rourke,
Kamila Shamsie, Bidisha SK Mamata, Karline Smith, Kim Squirrell,
Lucas Stewart & Eley Williams*

ISBN: 978-1-91269-707-6
£14.99

Refugee Tales: Volume III

Edited by David Herd and Anna Pincus

'A courageous book' – *Jackie Kay*

With nationalism and the far right on the rise across Europe and North America, there has never been a more important moment to face up to what we, in Britain, are doing to those who seek sanctuary. Still the UK detains people indefinitely under immigration rules. Bail hearings go unrecorded, people are picked up without notice, individuals feel abandoned in detention centres with no way of knowing when they will be released.

In *Refugee Tales III* we read the stories of people who have been through this process, many of whom have yet to see their cases resolved and who live in fear that at any moment they might be detained again. Poets, novelists and writers have once again collaborated with people who have experienced detention, their tales appearing alongside first-hand accounts by people who themselves have been detained. What we hear in these stories are the realities of the hostile environment, the human costs of a system that disregards rights, that denies freedoms and suspends lives.'

Featuring: Monica Ali, Lisa Appignanesi, David Constantine, Bernardine Evaristo, Patrick Gale, Abdulrazak Gurnah, David Herd, Emma Parsons, Ian Sansom, Jonathan Skinner, Gillian Slovo, Lytton Smith, Roma Tearne & Jonathan Wittenberg

ISBN: 978-1-91269-711-3
£9.99

All profits go to the Gatwick Detainee Welfare Group and Kent Help for Refugees.